ANGELA,
THIS "CONS
MAY NOT BE (
AS IT'S A L...

Oct
25/9/15

In The Wicker Wood

© **Pat Mc Namara**
writing as Lazarian Wordsmith
2015

This is a work of fiction – characters and events occurring only, in the imagination of the writer.

Chapter 1

It's life Jim: but not as we know it! The words kept running through his mind all the way back from the doctors appointment. He couldn't recall where or when he had heard the words, or why they had now come from deep in his memories, but the sentiments, that phrase was appropriate for him. Living with? No, not now! Dying with cancer was life, but not as he knew it.

The Doctor had been brief, professional in the way he delivered the news. "It's advanced colon cancer. An aggressive strain. Hard to control. No matter what we do, it's only a matter of time. But look on the bright side: you have time to put any affairs you have in order, time for a good holiday; perhaps that trip you always intended to take. You have some time, use it well. I would if it was me!"

Georgie hadn't listened. The words after cancer were lost, incomprehensible, garbled, not understood. Cancer! A death sentence! No hope! The words, the sentiments attacked him. Overwhelmed him. Contributed to the hot and at the same time cascading rivulets of cold perspiration that now erupted on his brow and back. He could feel some of it run down, inside his thigh, between the tweeds and his skin. Another quick panic seized him. He glanced down. Was it sweat? Had he pissed himself?

It's life Jim: but not as we know it: Star Trek. Ignoring the gestures and held-aloft messages, he marched through the front office, into his sanctuary at the back and sat behind his desk – Mister Spock! Doctor Mc Coy came to mind as well. "He's dead Jim!"

Taking the bottle from the desk drawer, he poured a large whiskey, gulped half of it down and felt it sting. Sting the blasted cancer, he thought. Burn the shagger. Burn him – just like – I'll be burning soon in Hell. He hadn't thought about the next life in a long time. But now he did it's impending closeness terrified him.

He poured another whiskey and drained it in one more gulp. He threw the glass at the wall. Hearing gasps from the outside office, he hastily called out "I dropped something. I'm off now for the day."

Milo's? Yes Milo's, a few more drinks, drown it, drown my thoughts as well! He needed to confess, to tell a confessor about the girls. Be absolved, be clean: save his immortal soul. He needed forgiveness: but how? If he told: he would lose: be disgraced, let the family name down. It would destroy all that they had built up over the years – over the centuries.

Chapter 2

Mistress Bowen was a descendant of a Scotch Presbyterian family who had been Planted into Ulster in 1689. Because of the tardiness of her various ancestors her branch of the family, over the years, had become cash poor. At twenty years of age, she was now in an arranged marriage.

She was determined to make her mark and preserve her individuality: as Mistress, in a large house, built in 1890, on the outskirts of the English Planted Town of Port Siney. Despite the influx of Huguenots that religious persecution in France attracted to the town, Mistress essentially regarded herself, the town, and her family as British.

She commanded a large staff of indoor and outdoor servants. All young and Irish and for the most part – in her view – feeble minded.

This led her to mistrust them and she came to believe they would benefit from regular confession and contrition: it would be good for their souls. In the extensive renovations of the house she had the confession box built and installed halfway along the landing.

She had watched over the local tradesmen who worked on the project until the box was in place. A tradesman from Dublin was recruited for the other special finishing: the spy seat in the hidden compartment. His task was completed by night. In the morning he collected his fee and departed on the canal barge that ferried Castlecomer Coal to the Capital. The household staff were never aware that he had been there.

From that time forward, the local Catholic curate was required to attend once a month, to hear confession and absolve the Catholic servants of their guilt.

The servants never questioned how after monthly confession, small items they had pilfered were found, or how those of them who had committed more serious transgressions were dismissed.

To them the confession box and their confessions, to God in there: were never suspected as the source of the information.

To Mistress Bowen, events occurring in her house were hers to know, and judge: their God could take care of their immortal souls after death. In life they were her servants and as such were bound by her rules.

In the middle of the Twenty Century, Georgie was raised in the house by Mumsie and Grammy. If he had been bold, Mumsie would take him to confessions. She would sit in the centre box, he sat in the side box and confessed his boldness. When satisfied, she forgave him and wiped away his tears. When he grew older – she said he grew bolder: the ritual happened nearly every evening. He sat in the box and told her about his day playing, or his day at school and the boys he met. One evening, just before she left, he confessed to her about the girls on the farm.

Her voice inside his head asked, Did you spill our seed George? He answered. No Mumsie. I didn't.

Chapter 3

Pubs in Ireland are places where, generally men, go to relax and shoot the breeze. This tabloid conversation is often not even remembered afterwards.

That was why Detective Fanahan liked Milo's. It was the place, where for example, himself and The Prick could have a discussion spanning their different religious beliefs.

It became a part of their pub conversation and was going on as long as they had been meeting for the end of week drink, or in the Detective's case, his end of shift until tomorrow session.

An argument about the rite of confession in the two religions began a long time ago when Fanahan, in one of his moods, first started teasing The Prick about not having to go to confession regularly: to tell his sins to a priest and receive absolution.

"Growing up we always envied you Proddie boys. You could take the girlfriend out for a night, drop the hand and grope her gee and never have to tell anyone you did it. You could just go away and forget about it. We had to go to bloody confession to get absolution before we could feel better. If you didn't go they had you so well conditioned: you were guilt ridden until you did go. If you told one of our lads that you got a handful of gee over a weekend, they'd hit the shaggin' roof. One head-banger asked me to send the little girl in to see him, so that he could have a talk with her."

When Mumsie and Grammy had been unsure of where exactly Georgie would eventually fit into Family Affairs – although the Major was unlikely to accept him as a true blood Bowen, they had hopes.

Instead of sending him to attend the local Protestant Schools, they placed him, out of the way: in the more distant Catholic School.

Georgie used the illicit knowledge of Religious Instruction gained there, to formulate and argue views designed to annoy Fanahan. Sometimes he even managed to see the anger in Fanahan, when one of his taunts struck home.

"Shay, if a man committed a murder and went to a priest and confessed and received forgiveness from God, no court of man could find him guilty, since a higher court, that of God, had forgiven him and in effect made him clean. Forgiveness is absolute whether it's for stealing sugar or murder. Once you have a firm resolution at the time of confessing, not to do the act again you would be forgiven. When you are contrite the priest has no option but to forgive you. Therefore what he binds on earth will be bound in heaven. You are clear with God and you guys are out of your jurisdiction."

Normally Fanahan would just laugh at this, but recently he was rising more to the bait and would get involved in an argument. "Look, as usual you are talking through your hole! When we went to school we had this kind of thing belted into us. Even now, I can still reel some of it off by heart."

In a deep sonorous authoritarian voice, he posed the question. "What is forbidden by the fifth commandment?"

In a childlike voice, the intoned reply. "It forbids murder and suicide and all other acts that inflict bodily injury on ourselves or on others. Now Georgie the next bit is for us."

Intoning again, he added, "What else is forbidden by the fifth commandment? The answer my boy is. It also forbids drunkenness, fighting, anger and revenge. And if you keep on at me like this I might have to break this commandment. While I'm at it and remembering, what about this one? When they were talking about the sixth commandment being a danger to chastity they made us learn that the chief dangers to chastity are: idleness, intemperance, bad companions like you - you Prick, improper dances, immodest dress, company keeping and again you and me indecent conversation, books, plays and pictures. These all make you want to be ridein' women, ridein' women; gettin' your hole; laying pipe; givin' her one; cleaning yer tubes. But there was never anything in there about rogering altar boys, was there?"

Tonight, when he arrived into Milo's, Georgie was there before him. He looked shook, in some distress: that put Fanahan into a good mood. Sensing that Bowen, might not be in the mood for a Philosophical Discussion, he launched straight in, with insults – even before the drink round had been called for.

"Well, my old accountant pal, have you spent all day in the office pullin' your wire and running an audit to check that your sperm count isn't diminishing? Give us the same again Milo. It's going to be a long night."

"No! It's my round Detective. Same again Milo. Make them doubles. I can only stay for one more. I'm on the five-fifteen home. Just in time for dinner and afterwards, well, I must confess, to tell the truth, I'm on a promise tonight."

Yea, thought Fanahan, elongating the name in his mind. *A promise with Paam and her five sisters!*

Georgie, was elated with his cleverness, aware that he was playing a dangerous game with a Detective Garda.

It's surprising how a sentence of impending death, can make you reckless- Mumsie.

Chapter 4

On the train journey home, Georgie took time again to reflect on the visit to the doctor earlier in the day. He was finished, that was for sure. No cure, no let up, no extensions of time, just a few months, then – the flames of Hell.

Long ago, he had come to the conclusion that if he could have catholic forgiveness, from a priest for his failings, for killing those girls who had wanted to go away and leave him, his soul would be clean and he would not rot in Hell.

Soon, he decided. I will kidnap a priest, start telling him about them. He will forgive me and God will have no option but to welcome me to Heaven. A firm purpose of amendment is all it takes : the promise not to sin again.

It was more complicated than that, because after over forty years on this earth, he was still unsure of who he really was? What made him tick? What drove him, motivated him, formed his character?

Of course he knew his name and his family name, but that wasn't who he was. It could never be as simple as that: a name, a place, a time, a family: that did not make you a person. It had no influence on who you really were, inside. If it had, surely he would not be in this situation, this mess.

If it was only as clear as that! George Edward Charles Bowen: last in a long line of the town Protestant Gentry. Owner of the big house, member of the Golf Society. Gentleman farmer, husband and father: then he might be happy, be content, perhaps even be sane.

It wasn't like that in any way at all. He was George E. Bowen, loser, unmarried, rattling around in an old house, unable to make a living from his fallow farm. He was a paid servant of others – accounter and balancer of their money and assets. He was also starting to believe Grammy when she told him that he was insane.

He had taken the first girl when he was twenty. He hadn't intend to: it just happened. He was driving, in those days. He saw her hitching a lift. He pulled in and picked her up. They talked student talk, she was so easy to speak with. When he reached the outskirts of the town, he stopped and let her out. He drove on, reconsidered and reversed back. He got out of the car. "Would you like to come up to the house and have something to eat before you travel on?"

She checked her watch: finding the idea interesting and trusting him, she agreed. When they reached the house Grammy had retired for her nap. They went to the kitchen and they had a nice afternoon: drinking tea, eating slices of brown bread and honey, talking, smiling and telling student stories.

That was the afternoon he fell in love with her and knew he wanted her to stay. When he put this proposition to her, she said she couldn't stay: she was expected home. She checked her watch again, said she was running a little late already and would have to leave. That was a pity – he suggested leaving her to the train station for a train home, that would make up for the delay. She said that would be nice.

He drove her to the station, paid for her fare and directed her to the platform. He left the station and walked up the stone stairway, to the road , to wave her off from the bridge. When he got there he saw that she was leaving the station. He ran back quickly to the car park, drove out and accosted her as she stood on the road. She had cashed in the ticket and was hitching again.

He accused her of lying to him, and taking advantage of his generosity. In a fury, he hit her and she fell to the path. No one had seen what happened, so he pushed her into the back seat of the car and drove quickly back to Bowen Court. When he got there he tied her up in the Ice House near the wood, went back to the house, said hello to Grammy and went to his room and cried.

He sobbed himself to sleep and dreamed of Mumsie. At three o'clock on that Summer morning just as the dawn chorus was beginning: still crying, still sad, still thinking of Mumsie, still feeling betrayed, he went to the Ice House, killed her and buried her in Sean's Willow Grove, beside the lake, in the middle of the wood.

Since he believed that everyone should have a marker for their final resting place: he carved her initials on a tree. He realized that for a proper burial with dignity he should say some words over her. He did not have a Bible, searching deep within his memory, he remembered the poem that sent him to sleep, when he was troubled, and Grammy would comfort him.

Winding wind whispering through white willows, over broken boughs of time-worn trees, lazily lapping their nearest neighbours brooding branches, in the eerie empty slumbering silence, of the Wicker Wood.

He was afraid, and had a sense of dread: he knew he would be found out and punished. That would also bring shame on the family.

For the next three days he remained in his room, listening to the radio, as the story of the missing girl broke, and the search began. He followed each false lead, his depression clearing as the clues led the searchers away from the Midlands. Concern deepening again, when someone reported that a girl answering the description of Paula Stafford had been seen on the Cork train at Port Siney. He knew this was not true, she had never boarded the train: if she had she would still be alive.

Over the next week the search tapered off and he began to relax. It was a terrible deed but it was behind him now and that was it: it was a mistake that must not happen again.

He often visited the grave and said he was sorry. Over time he decided that he could do this again and get away with it. If he could hide away a person that he had taken in daylight on the side of the street and kill them on the estate and bury them out of sight, where no one would ever look, he could do this again. This time if he planned it properly he would be safe: he would always be safe.

On that day as he returned to the house, through the trees, past the lake and up the privet walk he decided, I can recite some more of the poem for the next one.

She would not be lonely in the wood now, he had sent her more companions to keep her company: he did not want them to be as alone as he had been. Now there were eleven sets of initials on the tree. He sometimes stood there fingering the scars in the bark and remembering how all of them had been nice at first and how he loved all of them and how they all had betrayed him and wanted to leave

He had sin on his soul and he needed to confess. If a priest absolved them all would be fine. He could die safely – with a clean soul.

The voice inside in his head said, All fine and dandy Mumsie. She answered, All fine and dandy Baby.

Chapter 5

Georgie was pleased with himself. He had planned the capture of the priest with precision and it had all gone off without a hitch.

He had entered the church from the back and stood under the balcony. He located the confession box and the small queue, only three people. Two on the top side one on the bottom, two perhaps in the box. Therefore, he knew the session was not over and the priest was still inside. When he thought about abducting a priest from a confession box he reasoned that an attempt just at the end of the session would be best.

He waited: two out, two in, one remaining, the penitents moving away to the benches on the other side of the aisle or the centre benches of the church.

Now was the time, the priest would be relaxing knowing that his time of listening to these wretched people filling his mind with their filthy thoughts and deeds was nearly over for today.

He moved out from his cover and started to stride smartly up the aisle. He glanced down and his heart froze. He gasped audibly as he saw the dog lying just inside the pew. He had a hatred and fear of those animals, filthy flea infested shit buckets slobbering all over the place and fouling up the paths.

The dog rose and moved into the aisle. He decided to turn and run. The woman stood also and turned towards him blocking his escape. He panicked, he was going to fall, and the bloody animal would probably attack him as defenceless prey.

The woman said something and put out a hand towards him. Glad to make some human contact he reached forward and took hold of her arm, muttering some words of thanks and relief. The woman said "Sorry" and at the same time "It's OK" to the dog.

He stumbled free and found himself heading towards the Altar: away from the crossways to the confession box. *What is it they do as they cross the altar line? That's it down on the one knee, but which one? Do bloody both!*

He arose and moved to sit in the pews. Just the one person left. He waited. *Now! Now!* He stood, walked towards the box and knocked politely on the centre door.

"Father an accident! Down the street! They need a priest. I think he's dying. It's quickest out the back door!"

He heard the priest shuffle and close a shutter. He stepped out into the aisle, blinking in the sudden brightness and asking 'where' but instinctively turning to hurry down the aisle. Georgie followed closely. When they reached the yard and the priest saw the van waiting with the back doors already open – it was to late for him. A quick hard tap on the back of the head and a forward push and it was all over.

It only took a few seconds to secure and blindfold the captive and he was away motoring home. He smiled, great place churchyards: you can leave a van unattended with the engine running and it will be there when you come out.

When he reached home and had the priest safely locked away, he drove back to the city and dumped the van. Even this location was well chosen. He knew from past experience that the local kids, liked nothing better than to stand around, and throw cider cans into another burning car.

He went to the office and did a little auditing. At four o'clock he told the girls he would be away at meetings tomorrow and would see them again on Monday. He wished them a nice weekend and left to catch his train back home.

He was feeling so good that instead of the usual walk he took a taxi to the station. he could have a quick drink in Milo's, before the five-fifteen to Port.

Precisely at six-twenty he alighted from the train and was annoyed - as always to hear the porter call Port - Sin-eee, Port Sin-eee, all off for Port Sin-eee. "It's Port Siney!" He muttered.

He stood at the gates to the estate and considered once again what the family had built over the centuries. To his left was the village of cottages and two up - two down town houses, that had been built, to house the farm labourers and the mill managers and their families.

Originally it had been planned, built and named, by Eliam Troughton, as Troughtown. The local Irish who spoke Gaelic at the time began referring to the place as Trout Town or in their tongue Baile Breac, the town of the trout.

More confusion arose because trout in Ireland have various different markings and colour, from the vivid red spots of the Gillarue, to the almost pale shades of the Rain-bow breeds. The Gaelic name became Breac Cluain, the spotted trout. The village of Troughtown over time became Bracklone, or in the vernacular of the natives who could never pronounce words or names correctly - Bracklin Street.

To the right was the long Main Street terminated by the square, a street where even now the original Huguenot Style houses, with their wide semicircular approaches, their flights of entrance steps, and their extensive gardens stood firm: as monuments to their builders, even if some of the smaller houses were backside-on to the street, so built to minimize the window tax.

Across from the estate, on the hill, the Imperial Hotel turn-piked the trade area of the town.

He remembered the black cars that collected the travelling salesmen from the railway station each day, when the town was a prosperous Mecca of various shops: a flour mill, travel accessories - cases and trunks, hockey sticks and the ever popular Siney tennis racket. In the fifties the town had the first peat burning electricity generating station in the country.

He had been happy growing up here with Mumsie. At first there were others – Grammy and Gramps, although he could never call the Major that to his face,. It was Sir, or Major.

The rank had first been applied as a derisory one: when the older Bowen, fancying himself as protector of his estate, family and servants and even the town, founded a branch of the Local Defence Forces during the second World War.

The locals called him the Galloping Major as he raced his hunter through the streets each evening in search of subversives.

Afterwards when the L.D.F. was long disbanded he still used the rank and expected others to do the same. The Major was head of the house when George was young and ruled the family and the estate workers with strong will, strong rules and strong discipline.

He shivered in the dusk. At this time of year there can still be some frost. He noted a light in Grammys room as he walked up the drive to his flight of steps leading to his entrance.

You will have to wait My Dear. I have a chore to attend to – first.

Chapter 6

Jim Gaffney fell under the spell of the visiting Vocation Recruiter. When he was only fourteen years old, he was persuaded to leave the small Christian Brothers Secondary School in the West of Ireland and finish his education in the Seminary.

His mother was delighted: the dream of most Irish mothers was to have a priest in the family. His father was confused and told Jim that if he ever changed his mind, or as he really put it – came to his senses, a place would always be found for him in some business company in the town.

In his early twenties Jim was ordained. As an American Bishop had paid for his training, he was to start his work, in what his Father called 'The Mickey Mouse Ministry' Orlando Florida.

At his first meeting with his new boss, he was told what his duties would be: what the parish politics were, who to stay on the right side of, and was given the keys to his parish provided car. He was also bluntly advised, if he was going to fornicate, he should do so out of state and not to shit on his own doorstep.

Five years later, wiser, tanned and with an American Twang, not having travelled out of state a lot and still a virgin, Jim returned to Ireland. After some placements around the diocese, he now working in the western suburbs as curate in Saint Joseph's, an established and therefore busy parish.

He was hearing confessions after ten o'clock Mass on the Thursday morning before the Eve of First Friday, when the man called him out to an emergency.

It all happened so fast, so hurriedly, that he was lying in the back of the van handcuffed and with a hood over his head before he had recovered any of his composure.

He had no idea why anyone would abduct him. He hadn't got any real money, neither had his family: and the church would never pay to get him back.

After about an hour of being thrown around in the van, it stopped and he was roughly dragged out and instructed to stand. He was pushed, kicked and dragged a short distance and they entered a building and climbed upstairs, through some footfall echoing rooms. He was forced to fall on to a seat, in what he thought was a narrow storage room.

The handcuffs were removed, gloved hands also removed his watch, his diary and his pen. The door closed and he heard it being secured on the outside.

He pulled off the hood and as his eyes adjusted to the darkness his heart beat faster, a cold sweat chilled him, he was sitting in another confession box.

He remained imprisoned in the confession box for what seemed like several hours. He had tried to open the door, but could not find any handle or latch. As far as he could determine the door was smooth and he reasoned it was secured on the outside. The walls, roof and floor offered no escape either. Even bracing his feet against the door and his shoulders against the back wall and pushing with all the strength of his bent legs and arched body he could not move either the door, the back wall, or the box itself. He tried to prise open the wooden opening to the penitents part of the box, on both sides, with no success at all.

Finally the door on the penitents side was softly opened. He heard someone enter and shuffle into a kneeling position. He heard a click, once again he tried to slide back the wooden shutter and found that this time it opened. The smell of whiskey wafted in.

"Bless me Father, for I have sinned. This is my first confession,Father. I kidnapped a priest Father, but you know that."

The voice was cultured, not accented and soft and whispery. Jim could not detect any regional dialect or accent. If he had hoped he would find some clue to where he was, or who his gaoler was, he knew now he would not get it in this conversation.

"I took other people too, Father, several times. For these and all the sins of my past life, I'm truly sorry."

Before Jim could reply, or even jolt himself into confessional mode the voice said, "Put on the hood, its time for dinner."

The barked command brought him back to the absurdity of his position: not the priest in the sacrament of confession. A prisoner: in a confession box, somewhere, he believed, in the Irish Midlands.

Confused by the strange invitation, if that was what it was, he placed the hood over his head. Determined however to gain some advantage he did not pull it fully over his eyes and face immediately. The door was opened and strong light blinded him. Shocked he pulled the hood completely over his face and holding both door jambs pulled himself out. He was pushed and guided forward repeatedly until his progress was stopped by what he realized was the back of a chair.

"Sit down." He sat and his leg was shackled. "Wait.

Don't move. You are being watched. If you try to rise from this chair you will be shot." He heard a door behind him being opened. He sensed the man kneel, and felt movement at the bottom of his trouser leg "When I leave take off the hood. Keep looking straight ahead. Don't speak." He felt a breeze as the door was slammed.

He found himself sitting at one end of a long polished dining table. Silver candelabra placed evenly along the table provided a soft dim light. There were two settings. The one he was placed in front of: another at the top.

Close behind his chair a fire burned in a large fireplace. The smell of turf smoke reached him. The heat of the flames did not. Leaning sideways he looked beneath his char. He now wore a metal leg-iron. On the front side, above his ankle, it was secured by a padlock. Encircling the other side, below his calf : the noose of a slim steel rope held him tethered to an anchor point – out of sight, behind him.

The salad on the white dinner plate, reminded him that a single cup of tea and a little toast, had been his only meal this day.

In the house behind he heard the unmistakable sound of a clock bell-spring, winding its way to chime. The Westminster Chimes played the hourly salute. This was quickly followed by eight sonorous peals. If the clock was correct, it had been nine hours or so since he was lured out of the confessional.

As the echo of the final note died away, a figure descended from the last step of a corner stairway he had not noticed, and walked slowly to the other dining place. He was expecting his captor.

A tall straight backed oldish, grey-haired lady, stepped into the candle light. She was dressed in a black dress complete with bustle. She moved to her chair and stood mute, gazing intently at him down the length of the table: waiting. Unbidden by words, only by the gaze, he stood.

She bowed slightly, moved to the chair and sat down. Jim sat again. She looked up, folded her gloved hands across her breast and spoke. The voice was clear and strong.

"Will you say the grace Pastor?" She enquired. Astonished Jim complied.

She ate slowly with deliberation. Occasionally she raised a napkin to her lips and wiped away imaginary food scraps or digestive juices. Finally she used the napkin, one last time, pushed back her chair and stood. He rose and she turned and walked slowly into the alcove stairway and left.

Jim turned from the table, grasped his restraint and pulled the cable. It resisted stretched tight, held beneath and outside the heavy door.

He yanked again, this time jerking it from side to side. Once again it held firm. He threw the cable down and tried to open the door. It was locked and secure, strong and unbreakable. He went back and tried to lift the chair, he sat in during dinner, it was fixed to the floor.

In desperation he took his plate and flung it: to crash and shatter against the door. He heard a voice from outside order him to behave, or suffer the consequences.

He defiantly roared "Feck OFF!"

The voice asked again if he was going to behave himself.

"No!" He screamed. "Feck OFF!"

Only silence greeted his defiance.

After some time he was asked again, and his answer was the same blasphemy.

Some hours later, as the early morning light turned the dark into grey shadows. The birds woke to call the dawn. When he could no longer stand the cold and the dark, the pain in his leg – where the anklet tore at his flesh, as he paced, and the isolation: he agreed, when asked again, that he would behave himself.

The voice, more distant now than before, instructed him to open the door, follow the rail and sit in the confession box. The hall was brighter, lit by the long coloured, stain-glass-window, set high into what he thought was an East facing wall. He moved to the box and sat into his customary centre seat. He heard a low cough and he pulled back the shutter. It opened easily.

Through the grill the whispering voice instructed. "You will be confined in your rooms, at the end of the hall – they have toilet facilities – each day. You will remain there until evening. When the clock plays the three-quarter-hour chimes, after six o'clock: you will follow the guide rail to this confessional. You will enter and wait for me. You will hear my confessions. When I am finished you will wait until the chimes mark the next three-quarter hour. At that time you will leave the box and follow the rail and enter the room and take your place for dinner. On the quarter hour chime after dinner you will follow the rail again and return to your room. This will be your daily task. At times, I will require you to perform other duties. When this happened I will inform you of these tasks: after daily confession. Wait now here, until you hear the next chime, then exit."

Without thinking of the consequences of meeting his captor, face-to-face, Jim pulled open his door, leaped out and turning, wrenched open the door on the penitents side. Adrenaline pumping, hands clenched – he was prepared to jump into the stall: to kick and fight, for his freedom, and his life. At that precise moment, Jim Gaffney confessor and priest, would have killed.

His eyes adjusted to the dimness inside. He saw small red and green indicator lights blinking: in tune with the laughter transmitted from a device.

I saw one in America! It was being used to listen to a baby sleeping! Big Brother is watching me!

He stepped back. He was on a narrow landing about ten yards long. The box was about seven feet high, with a confessor stall, and a right and left penitent stall. The hall that led to his room and the dining room was also narrow.

At the side wall a rail was fixed close to the floor. It looked like a single miniature train track. Jim bent: it was rigid and held by square end plates. They were secured by bolts, stud-end uppermost, that went into the floor to their companions, the real holding plates, with the nuts beneath.

His leg iron and cable were fastened to the rail by what looked like an upside down, small, two-pronged garden fork. It was captured by the rail, yet could move along it. Jim pulled with all his might on the fork and the cable but both held firm. The doors were modified, to allow his hawser pass beneath.

He kicked the rail in several places and jumped on top of it, but again it did not yield.

This rail and where it allowed him move to, or go to, was going to be his world for the future.

He heard the Westminster Chimes strike.

He turned and dragging his 'rail and chain' behind him entered his quarters.

Chapter 7

Shay Fanahan thought the first situation briefing had gone well except for the smart questions from that cute Cavan Hoor Superintendent Tyrell. Had they checked for fingerprints in the confessional box? Wasn't the shaggin' thing walking with shaggin' fingerprints, with half the knackers and whores in Dublin in there every day, pouring out their filthy lives to the stupid clergy.

The facts were clear as day. A feckin' nut case walks into the Church. Gets the priest out of the confessional. Marches him out into a blue, green or dark van, depending on which Missus you interviewed, and away they go.

The other stupid auld biddies eating lumps off the altar rails didn't see a thing, except to say they thought the man had called the priest away to an emergency, an accident perhaps. A fire one thought. What did she think the priest could do? Piss on the fire!

There was no other witness except the other blind biddy with the white cane and the guide-dog. Unless the shaggin' dog could talk: she wasn't worth interviewing at all.

In the next few hours, every feckin' bishop and even an Archbishop, or two, would be on the phone, or faxin' their disgust at the slow progress.

All of them would be under pressure from the friggin' politicians for a quick fix.

The drunken drivers would have a feckin' terrible time with all the feckin' patrols. *Serves them right! The shaggers!*

He was away now to talk to the dope heads, and the winos and the filth on the streets and with a bit of luck he would kick a confession out of some poor bollix. Or if the priest would oblige by turning up dead somewhere, they could hand the case to the murder squad, and all this would go away quickly.

Fanahan wasn't having much success kicking arse. His informants were dumber than usual and no amount of threats or bribes could bring out information they hadn't got.

At five feet eight he was small for the force. He had enlisted during a height amnesty, when Garda recruitment was going through a slump, due to bad pay, a bad press and strict discipline.

At first he progressed quickly through the uniformed ranks to his position now as a detective with the rank of Sergeant. He blamed his recent lack of advancement in the Inspector Examination and interview, to the influence of that bloody shower who were the current Government party.

Feck it! He thought, it's nearly tea time and I need a drink. He headed toward Kingsbridge and for Milo's Tavern the ale house he had given his custom to, since he arrived in Dublin, off the Galway train.

"Good afternoon you shower of Muppets" he shouted as he entered the dark comforting atmosphere.

The pub was currently owned by a retired farmer, who having drank dry, or worn out his welcome, in the local pubs in County Meath, had sold the large farm for development potential.

With Euro millions Milo had moved to the city and was now working on drinking out his own premises. Fanahan often wondered would the money, the drink, or the liver give up first.

"The usual" he said, almost to late, as the Jameson and the Guinness arrived together. Drinking the whiskey in one gulp and following it with a large cooling chaser from the pint – he began his usual put-down banter. "Hey there Theo. What's Tommie's last name?"

Theo, the worse for wear having been on the batter for a few days, slipped up, and in confusion, not sure of what he had heard, asked, "Tommie who?"

"So he's a Chinaman, then, is he?"

"Wha'?"

"Tommy Hu! Jees forget it."

Bob Tyrell had been summoned to call and brief Bishop Mahon at The Palace. In his heart he had always been expecting some nut somewhere, to attack, kill or abduct a priest.

The Church in the Casey affair and the Fortune and Payne cases and their reaction to the Tribunal, never really got to grips with what the man in the street wanted: retribution, justice, contrition, admission, and future protection.

Tyrell at forty-five was a lifer in the police force, the Gardaí, the Guards. At six foot four in height, he was now getting just a few pounds over what he regarded, as fighting fit weight. He was still however muscle hard and could move almost as fast as ever, thought not fast enough or hard enough any more, for the Gaelic fields.

As he entered the sitting room Bishop Mahon raised a cut-glass whiskey tumbler and a bottle of Jameson, motioned towards the chair and said, "Sit down Bob. Will you have a drink?"

Almost as an after thought he added, "No, I remember now you don't drink or smoke. Unusual for a policeman I always thought."

"Thank you your Grace," Tyrell replied, dropping into a well-polished Victorian Grandfather Chair. The rich red velvet upholstery setting off the blue-grey of his uniform.

Mahon took his wide squat well-filled glass of amber whiskey and relaxed into the companion Grandmother chair. He swirled the ice and the spirits, loaded his mouth, swallowed, drew a deep breath and began. "Bob, this curate is clear as far as my investigations go. No suspicions at all, no women, no drink, no gambling. It's very strange that he should be lifted like that." The bishop's language sometimes dropped back into the vernacular of his days as a go-between in the peace process.

Bob was also at a dead-end to explain the reasons. His investigation agreed with this assessment. A straight young curate intent only, it seemed on his priestly duties, and on the good of the people in his spiritual care, had been spirited away. He had no leads to go on. There appeared to be no motive. He had no suspicions of anyone at all.

"Your Grace" Bob began.

"Now Bob. You know I prefer Bishop."

"Bishop. We have no clues, no trail to follow. Some of our best men are out now, starting to question known criminals, and their associates. I'm sure before long we will have a lead."

"Who have you, on the team Bob? Good men?"

"We have Tom Ryan, from the Crumlin shop. Aidan McGill, he's new, just up from Donegal. They say he's a good foot soldier, and from my squad, Shay Fanahan…"

"The Lugs admirer?" Mahon raised one quizzical eyebrow and looked squarely at Bob.

Bob remembered how the urban legend had begun when Fanahan was asked a question at a Community Gardaí forum.

'If a Leprechaun gave you three wishes what would they be?' Immediately, tongue in cheek, Fanahan replied. 'Three nights on the town, with Lugs Branigan and his patrols against street nuisances, back in the fifties or sixties. Lugs knew how to enforce the rule of law!'

"Yes."

To his relief the bishop changed tack. "Has Ryan's leg healed?"

"He still carries a few pellets, but he's getting there."

Trying to wrestle control of the conversation back from the barked questions Bob added. "It's a fine team. I'm sure they will get quick results."

"With the help of God, Bob." Mahon replied as he stood up. Turning his back, he moved to stand and stare out the window, and deliberately drained his glass in one quick swallow.

With that the interview was over. The housekeeper had appeared as if by psychic summons at Bob's elbow. Making his goodbyes he left.

As he walked towards his car he noticed the grandeur of the tree lined avenue and the immaculate lawns of the Bishops Palace. He looked back: but the bishop was no longer at the window.

"Almost another world" he remarked as he found his keys and disengaged the alarm and the central locking. "Why do I bother?"

Out of sight, having moved from the windows, Mahon filled his glass with a big measure of whiskey and sat down to think.

The priest was no danger to him. The kidnapper, who ever he was, could not be either.

It was just the whole episode – it could get out of hand. He would have to show he could manage this, could call in favours and get it sorted. Prove he was still a player.

If he could get this all fixed, quickly, no fuss, no blood spilled: the priest handed over to him in some isolated spot, just like the old days – maybe the Red Hat would come soon.

He fished his Fob Watch and chain from his waistcoat pocket and opening a compartment at the back took out a small key. He went to his desk, removed the middle drawer and reaching in used the key to open the hidden drawer.

He took out some documents and selected a small address book.

By the time Bob Tyrell was back in his office, Mahon was renewing old acquaintances, with his contacts along both sides of the border with Northern Ireland.

Chapter 8

She met him for the first time on a trip to Lourdes. She was
a pilgrim with the Armagh Diocese. He was with the Irish
Army Pilgrimage. She was in Lourdes with her mother: who
was in the final stages of her terminal cancer.

This place of pilgrimage in the south of France, was
often the final avenue of hope, for so many Irish who had
faith in the mercies of Our Blessed Lady. To visit the Grotto
in Lourdes was for many; a final attempt to find the peace of
mind to accept the illness, and it's ultimate ending.

Or a place of intercession where the Mother of God
would influence her son – so that the healing – so fervently
prayed for would be received.

Each evening, when the ceremonies were completed
and when Mother was delivered back to the carers in the
Hospice, she returned to her lonely room in the Hotel Padua.

Each morning, at seven o'clock, the massed ranks of
the Army Pilgrimages paraded from their camp higher up
the hill, past her hotel and down to the Grotto.

In her third floor room she waited straining to pick up
the first sounds of the marching feet. She would move out to
the balcony and admire the colourful march-past.

Each country had its own flags, battalion, platoon and
army colours. To a girl, who normally awoke to the sounds
of the creamery truck, and the voices of her brother and the
driver exchanging, weather, crop, and parish gossip: it was
like Hollywood.

She lived in an area of small county farms, in a community
where everyone knew each other. It was a sheltered place

where families were content to work the land in isolation as their people had done for generations.

It was a place where family names and given names were blended into the descriptive names of the time and language of a time when this settlement community in Ulster was first know as The People from Connaught.

She was Tom's-Maire McEntaggart, to distinguish her from Sean's-Maire Mc Entaggart.

Her cousins the MacGowans were known as Thorlough's-Mick and Mick's-Mick and Sean's-Mick after their fathers who in their time had been similarly adorned with kit and kin callings.

Wednesday in Lourdes, was the day when up in the town at the Hotel Astoria, Serge the owner hosted his usual midweek tea-party. They were all invited. After Mother was handed into the care of the Hospice for the night, she put on her good brown suit and in the company of some members of her own pilgrimage, they walked down the town, across the river and up towards the old town: to the Astoria.

Since Serge had as usual, shrewdly extended the invitation to the other pilgrims, in most of the other hotels, the Astoria was doing good business, when they arrived.

Not being forward or pushy, she held back when her companions went to look for spaces, at some of the less crowded tables.

She saw them gesture and went forward to stand beside a table already occupied by five men. A tall slim, by far the best looking man, older than his companions, dressed in black slacks and black open necked shirt, moved inward on a bench and invited her to sit beside him.

She sat. Both groups introduced themselves.

We're with the Armagh they offered. Army Officers, with the Irish up in the camp. In civvies tonight: out to relax. The older man suggested that he would organize a round of drinks. She did not want to reveal her ignorance of pub culture so said she was on wine also, just like her friends. White she agreed would be fine.

He left and came back accompanied by a waiter who arranged two bottles of white wine, five bottles of beer and what looked like five spirit drinks on the table. "No charge," he replied when asked. "Serge says they are on him."

In the next hours as the night filled with a deep darkness, flickering moths waved in and out of the table candlelight and the sounds of the Old Town softened into sleep, she drank the wine, danced with, was infatuated by, and fell instantly in love with Francis Sylvester Mahon.

Later still: towards morning, they walked swaying, laughing, giggling, arms and bodies entwined, back to her hotel and to her room.

He was her first lover. The tenderness of the early enticing kisses: the fondling beneath her blouse and the finger inserted to tease and flick at her hardening nipple; the tenderness with which he undressed her, contrasted with the roughness, the pain of her penetration, and the selfishness and brevity of the consummation.

Her sense of shame, sin, and guilt afterwards, seemed to find a fellow-feeling in him. He dressed quickly and left quickly mumbling words of sorrow, of shame and apology, even guilt and she sensed - fear.

Her head hurt, her body hurt, her feelings hurt: slantwise images of the night replayed in her head until they were blocked out by the need to sleep; the images continued as unwelcome dreams.

In the morning even the beat of marching morning feet failed to rouse her and she arrived late to collect Mother from the Hospice.

She saw him later in the morning: in the plaza beneath the church. She waved but he turned his uniformed, tall slim figure, his black shirt, his Roman Collar and his chaplain's insignia, from her and walked away to be quickly swallowed up and hidden in the camouflaging ranks of his parishioners.

In the months that followed the cancer conquered her mother, and she claimed her birthright in the family plot in the cold boggy soil, of an Ulster churchyard.

Her father cried his un-wet tears and walked the fields to meet his silent grief alone. The baby, hidden deep within her dumpy body, and her bulky farm work clothes, grew, kicked, moved, and nagged constantly at her shame.

She had picked her nest of birthing in the meadow beside the flax hole in the lower field, in the shadow of the mountain near the Carbane Sun-Mounds. She would have their baby there at the place of final rest. She knew this baby was a boy and when she had delivered him she planned to drown him and herself in the murky bog water.

Their time came and the pain was deep and hard and long. Her body and mind cried for relief. She prayed to her God to forgive her and to help her – for this cup to pass from her too. However she knew she must endure this anguish because she had tempted His priest into sin.

When the pain was a searing knife deep within her body and mind and her anguish was greatest, she heard a quiet comforting voice beside her. In her native Gaelic language she heard her father. "Easy, easy, I'm here, hold my hand. I will take the pain, it's fine, there is no shame in giving life. It's a good natural thing."

Afterwards, he took her son, his grandson, and washed him with gently hand lapped, palm cradled, sparkling water splashes, dried him in his shirt and raising him gently towards the heavens. He asked softly. "Who will name this child?"

He waited. Turning the child to the four winds, he asked again, gently, softly, quietly. "Who will name this child?"

After the fourth asking he waited again and raising his voice, in the language of his Connaught youth, of his father and forefathers before him: he answered. "I will name this child. I name him Tomás McEntaggart."

He returned from the flax hole and gently placed the child in her arms.

"The people around will shortly find a name for him. So we will call him Sonny."

Satisfied, finding a refreshed strength within himself, this hidden man, who first gave her life and now gave her son a name, and protection, lifted them and crying wet tears carried them home.

The boy grew and was know in the district as Sonny McEntaggart.

When he was on the run, the covert assassination file built up by the informer, named him as Thomas alias Sonny McEntaggart. When he met Ahab, in the IBIS hotel in Amsterdam, he was calling himself Shane O'Neill.

Chapter 9

He sat in the cafe at the corner of Dam Square, sipped his beer and watched the people who boarded and alighted from the trams, at the stop outside. It was early and apart from three elderly matrons: well dressed, well made up, well adorned with jewellery and obviously well heeled, he was alone.

He had been surprised to get the message from Ahab, more surprised at the request to meet in Amsterdam. It had been a long time.

When he was an IRA commander in Ulster and Ahab was a go-between from the Republic. They had worked together, whenever serious negotiations on kidnapping or hostages, required secret meetings, and quick action that would reflect well: on both the IRA and the Law Enforcement Agencies in the South.

Shane owed Ahab a favour, It was Ahab who tipped him off, that the British Security Forces had run him to earth in South Armagh, and were about to close in. O'Neill had no doubt that in the planned operation – he would be shot while trying to escape.

He had made his way to Amsterdam and espoused his new cause, of drug running back to Ireland, as passionately as he had once espoused the cause of a United Ireland. It was better paid and more regular work. For the most part the job was safer, since in his daily activities now, very few people were lying in wait: trying to shoot him.

Ahab came from the direction of the Canal and the Red-light district, moved across the front of the Krasnapolski Hotel and stood to admire the Royal Palace.

If I didn't know you, Ahab me boy, I would be fooled by that manoeuvre, O'Neill thought. Not satisfied by what ever he had observed, Ahab turned, accosted a passer-by and appeared to ask directions, then moved back in the direction on the Canal, towards the bridge and away from the Square. "Cautious Bastard" O'Neill muttered, "asking the way to where you came from, not where you are heading to."

O'Neill beckoned to the waiter, pointed at his empty glass and with an invisible pen poised, wrote in the air. He had thirty minutes to enjoy his solitude, before he needed to leave, and walk towards the secondary meeting place.

When he arrived in the lobby of the IBIS Hotel beside Central Station, Ahab was already seated in the bar with a large whiskey and ice, on the table.

"A Chara" he said in Gaelic as O'Neill sat down, "I'll have the same again."

After some small talk about Ireland, the flight, the breakfast on board and the Bucks Fizz, Ahab opened the real conversation.

"Shane I have a favour to ask. I have a small problem, a man with your talents and contacts, may be able to help me with. Someone lifted a priest out of the Westpark church in the Dublin Parish – my parish. He took him away in a van and now they're gone and there are no clues, no trace of him or the abductor, or the van burned out somewhere, and the local half-yards can't get on the trail at all. I need to know who lifted him. Was it one of your old friends? Or the new players in the game, the unofficial boys, or some of the local heavy gangs? I have a personal interest in this. I don't want any boyo shittin' on my doorstep and getting away with it. Can you put out some feelers and if you find out anything I would be forever grateful."

In case there was any misunderstanding, he added. "It would make us quits."

Catching the attention of a passing waitress: he pointed at the table and made a circular motion with his left hand, "The same again."

Turning to Shane he said, "It's a nice city, easy to get to from Dublin. Plenty of activity, I enjoy coming here. Send a message through channels if you get any news, see what you can do. We'll finish this round, and you can buy me a drink for the road, and I'll be away to the airport."

Chapter 10

Anto Byrne was surprised when The Boss rang him in person. He had been working for over a year collecting the consignments from the mules, and getting it into the distribution chain, in the flats around the city.

In all that time, he had never spoken with his big boss, just acted on the directions contained in the regular messages, he received from his own contact. He felt good, important, that he had been entrusted with this personal matter. He would do all in his power to see if in any way he could winkle out any information on who was holding the priest.

Maybe, if he succeeded, he would move up in the organization and be allowed run a few mules of his own. That was the way to real money, being able to pocket more of the cash, than he was doing at present.

What Anto didn't know was that he was only one of several people, who were working on this personal favour, for O'Neill.

What he didn't realise, either, was that he already had most of the answer.

To supplement his earnings, Anto was always on the look out for some quick money. Some nixer that would add to his capital. One day it was going to be enough: to let him buy a good big stash of drugs, and sell it for a big profit.

When he had achieved this he would be on his way. Maybe to being one of the drug barons. The Millionaires of the Dublin underworld.

He would have real capital – he liked that word. He had first heard it used, when he delivered his own small consignment, to his contact in the accountant's office.

Anto figured she passed it on at a profit, to her spotty friends for the weekends. He didn't care as long as she got her drugs from him, and recently, he had needed to spill more to keep up the supply.

The van was not going to get him great money. A couple of hundred squids was better that nothing. If that big accountant bollix in Croft Square, from the same bleedin' office, was stupid enough to leave it under his nose in the flats, then he was going to steal it.

"Why the Feck," he asked the watching walls, "would an accountant dump a van: instead of selling it? It can't be hot. I know! He left it for the kids to burn out. Must be some insurance scam for a client."

Shane had learned, a long time ago in Ulster, that the success of any operation depended on how good his watchers were, those people he used: to spy on all the others, and report back only to him. He had added a refinement of his own to this trusted order of business – he employed people to watch his snoopers.

When Anto lifted the van, his watcher, being that little bit smarter than Anto, asked himself the right questions and got the right answers.

Why would a so-called respectable accountant dump this van where it would be quickly burned out?

Because he was not as respectable as it seemed and he wanted it burned out.

Watcher had the bones, the weekend papers gave him the flesh.

Chapter 11

Traonach delivered the report. Anto was ripping the business off above the acceptable tilly. He was calling it spillage and setting up his own runs: to his own clients. He had a sidekick now a girl, a user, and he was supplying her for sex and to keep her around to beat the shit out of now and then. That was dangerous – because once the supplier becomes his own customer, all the rules change.

She was a liability for Anto and Anto was a liability to the operation in Ireland.

O'Neill suspected he also had the information Ahab needed, the accountant either was the kidnapper, or was working with the kidnapper. He would need a little more information, a little more proof, before he acted.

On the Anto front he had all the proof, and clues, he wanted. Even if he was totally wrong, it would be a lesson both for Anto and any other bollix, with ideas of taking advantage. It was a long time since he practised his punishment skills.

If he did not deal with this problem real soon, he could lose his business to some Dublin criminal who reasoned he had gone soft, and would move in while he was a Continental Absentee Landlord.

He would have to try and see his mother and grandfather too. That would be very dangerous, but there were still questions he needed answered. Time was quickly running out for all of them. He would have to risk a trip to Ireland. The operation needed sorting and Anto needed a good thumping.

He had other problems to sort first. He had to ensure

he would be safe and that he could get in and out unnoticed. It would cost a lot for Billy the Blade to provide him with a new identity, but it would cost more if this cock-up was not sorted.

The photograph looked a little like him, enough like him not to arouse suspicion if viewed on entry to Ireland. Enough unlike him, so that a nosy immigration official or cop, would not link the likeness with a previously wanted and listed terrorist.

I wonder who was Pádraig Nolan and what Amsterdam canal is he at the bottom of now?

On a trip like this a real passport, real credit cards: not for use just for cover, and a wallet with all the usual inserts was essential. He had no time for being pulled in for questioning, if any checks were carried out the plan would come apart.

It's always darkest under the light, he preached the message constantly: be invisible, be unobtrusive, be faceless. It had served him well in the past; it would not let him down now.

He got off the Frankfurt to Cork and Dublin flight in Cork and travelled to Dublin by train. From there he took a locally run country bus and was in his home place, in the shadows of the Carbane Mountains, by evening. His mother was surprised, happy to see him, but anxious and worried.

Why didn't you stay where you were. I'd rather have you over there alive, than dead above in some field on the mountain: her usual advice.

As before he replied - I had to see you Ma. Neither of us will ever know when it's for the last time.

She was not that old, but she looked broken now with all the burdens she had carried for him, trying to raise him in a locality where she imagined that everybody knew her story. She felt they also knew the shame she endured daily from her own conscience.

She had never told Sonny the whole story, just fobbed his inquiries off with the reply - foolishness and youth, and lack of control, and first time away beyond a mile from a cowshite.

She looked at her son the freedom fighter: some would say a terrorist. They were the people who had never lived with the real terror of sectarianism of being hated because of the religious belief you were born into. Maybe ones you no longer held or believed, but were still tarred with.

He looked older but not as strained as before. There was something on his mind. She hoped violence was not a part of whatever solution he had in mind. She had all the violence she could bear.

He looked around, out through the window, towards the fields, towards the mountain, searching.

"He's not here any more," she said before his question. "He's away above in the Home. They put him in there when he started rambling in his mind, said I would not be able to look after him, at home here."

With ice in his voice he asked, "Who's they?"

"The Health Board."

Again icily, "Who from the board? Shanley?

"No, he's gone, retired. A new fellow down from Dublin: Shanley would have left him here." A few tears welled up in her eyes. "I tried to keep him here, I could have nursed him, I nursed Mammy. I did, so I did."

"Can I go up and see him? Are there hours when you

can visit?"

"Anytime" she replied. "You can go anytime, but what if someone sees you, recognizes you, what will you do?"

"Is Patsy still around?"

"Yes, I'll go and get him. He will organize you safe there and back."

Her step was lighter as she put on her coat and prepared to leave. "Yes! Patsy will see you safe. So he will."

Chapter 12

Patsy softly closed the door to the day-room behind him. He had carried out his duty. He had delivered Sonny into the Home, without incident. He put the keys back into his overall pocket and pointed, "There he said, in the chair by the window, that's him."

O'Neill went forward and squatted by the chair. He reached forward and touched his Grandfather's elbow. A face he did not know, with eyes blank, staring and dead, turned towards him.

"Daideo," he began in Gaelic, "It's Sonny."

Daideo turned blankly, not seeing, struggling to make the mental links, that would make him see. His mouth moved. O'Neill leaned closer.

"Mind her. Mind your mother." His head dropped down again and he examined the floor. "The sins of the fathers," he muttered. "She came back, full of the sin of that father, but I never blamed her, or the boy"

Patsy crept forward. "Make it short Sonny. Time is ticking."

O'Neill waved a dismissive hand. "Quiet! "I can't make out what he's saying. Daideo, I'm here! It's me Sonny. Daideo!"

Daideo reached out and grabbed his arm. "Sonny? Is it you?"

"Yes Daideo. It's me Sonny, I'm here."

"She never wanted to tell you. I did. She kept a tin: a Billy-Can, to show you, to tell you. She threw it away: into the flax-hole. I marked the spot and got it out. I dried them in the sun. Hid them, below the third stone on the mountain

– the Druid's Stone. The hay will be good this year. I'll turn it with the rake and bring it home on the bogie. Mind them children there! Who owns them?"

He sat muttering, and sobbing softly in the midst of some inconsolable memory, distraught, his mind lost in the past and destined to remain there.

For him there was no today, no tomorrow: only yesterdays.

Sonny knew the spot. In his day it had hidden more than a round tin can. He drew it out. It was still black with the stains of turf fires and spilled brown tea, milked, with the sugar already added.

It's the one we used for boiling the water for the tea on the bog.

It was a good can, made well, with outside lugs for the handle, especially made, for it's job – as a Bog-Billy-Can.

It had weathered well: with only a little rust at the bottom seam. O'Neill dug deeper and disturbed the bed of stones laid long ago to drain the hole and protect the can from the worse ravages of lying water.

Daideo, always the tradesman approach, always the finish, to make the job last longer.

He opened the snug lid and reached inside. Withdrawing amber fading photographs and yellow newspaper clippings. One photograph was of his mother very young with another girl and three men, at a table well stocked with drink and glasses at a party, somewhere lost in the past.

Another was a Lourdes Pilgrimage Photo, a stock local photographer's record, of the visit of the Armagh Pilgrimage.

His mother and grandmother ringed in pencil side-by-side: smiling.

The next photograph puzzled him. It was a similar record of the Irish Army Pilgrimage to Lourdes, in the same year.

A figure at the side was ringed in pencil. A line with an arrow at its tip came from this circle and pointed at the initials F.S.M. He looked closer, lifting the picture to the evening sun.

The man in uniform was wearing a Roman Collar – an Army Chaplain.

He quickly checked the other fading photographs and cuttings, as they traced the career of Francis Sylvester Mahon from his Army career, to his appointment as a bishop in the Catholic Church.

An uneasy chill shook his body: Ahab.

The last paper in the middle of the rolled cone of clippings was a copy of his own birth certificate.

In the space he had viewed so often before: when he delivered it to the sneering priests in preparation for First Communion, and Confirmation. Where it normally said 'Father Unknown': there was now a correction in pencil. The faded writing, in his mother's unmistakable hand, read Francis Sylvester Mahon.

Chapter 13

His prison was a long stone built room that at this time of
the year, in the changeable weather – would be to hot or to
cold. It had two alcoves: one at some stage had perhaps been
a kitchen, the other a storage room, now serving as a toilet
and wash area. Each had a small window, barred and
boarded on the outside.

When Jim pushed one eye up to the cracks between
the boards, he could see glimpses of a garden, overgrown
and unattended.

By standing on the toilet and pushing his head and
neck into the ceiling, in a cramped and agonizing position,
almost kissing the side wall, and turning his right eye in a
painful, tear producing downward glance, he thought he
could make out a porch, leading out into the garden from beneath his floor.

After more exploration he came to the conclusion, that
from the stout wood floor beneath his feet, to the white-
washed ceiling above – he was confined to the first floor of
a stable, or out-office. Moreover he reasoned that from his
door to the end of the confession box, the narrow hall, was a
connecting passageway to the main house.

His room containing a bed bolted to the floor and the
side wall. At the other end the chimney was blocked somewhere high up inside and offered no chance of escape.

On the second and third day of confinement, he heard
whinging confessions that told him nothing: they were of the
"I robbed sugar Father" variety.

The absolution however was received with an audible
sigh. For some reason Jim knew that receiving forgiveness

and believing that his soul was clean in the eyes of God was important for his captor. This he felt could be an advantage and he determined to play the only card he held, so far in this game, carefully and as timely as possible.

When he entered the dining room: his food awaited him in covered serving dishes. Some kind of stew – not over endowed with flavour. The meal was eaten in silence.

His shackle and the rail allowed him to go only as far as his place setting. His hostess at the other end was free to come and go as she pleased. It was obvious to Jim that she was the lady of the house, and in some weird way that he was the visiting cleric.

The meal lasted one hour and then The Duchess: this was how Jim now thought of her, left.

Before she departed she would motion for Jim to take the waiting after-dinner brandy, then rise and wait pointedly for him to stand also. At that stage, she would without any haste, leave the room.

After her departure he would have a few minutes alone before he was expected to return to his own room.

One evening, just as she had left the table, she stopped and turned slightly. "I hope the accommodation is to a standard you approve of Parson." Without waiting for a reply she turned and left the room.

Jim was so surprised by the performance; that in no way afterwards could he remember an accent, a speech af-fection, or any other distinguishing clue. The episode was just a lady, inquiring in old fashioned polite conversation, if he was happy with his digs.

If he had been quick enough he might have replied Not as accommodating as I would wish, Ma'am.

He decided to be prepared for any more sudden

speeches, so that he could reply and perhaps catch her off guard and learn something: that might be to his advantage.

At the next opportunity, Jim told his penitent in confession that he would be unable to offer absolution unless the sinner was bodily present, to receive it.

He knew it was vital to win this point. If the abductor was able to control the sessions remotely – any advantage that might be gained by a physical presence would be removed. Escape, or the gathering of information that might assist an escape, would be more difficult.

The session ended when Jim made this demand. He waited expecting retribution, and was surprised when he was able to train-rail to dinner and on the appointed time. Then afterwards to walk back to his room: without incident.

The next day he made the journey to the box without hearing any confession, his captor did not appear, either in person, or remotely. He attended his evening meal with the Duchess.

When he returned to his room, he noticed that the baby monitor was now in his room.

Chapter 14

Just before he retired for the night the whispering voice informed him that there would be no requirement for him to hear confession – in the immediate future.

Jim had a fitful sleep: wondering if his ruse had backfired, that now he was no longer required, and was expendable.

The following morning he was instructed to remain in his room. There would not be a breakfast.

To Jim's relief, in the evening the whispering voice ordered him, to attend dinner. During this meal Jim relaxed a little. If he was going to be killed his captor would have done so, during the day.

On the next morning the disembodied voice instructed him to attend for confession again – to the chimes signalling the half hour after six, this evening.

When Jim entered the confession box and sat down, he noticed a new addition. A large circular ring was fastened to the inside of the door. When he moved onto his bench, a thick wooden beam was inserted into this ring and across his door.

He could hear his personalized confession now but he was confined to the box and controlled by the penitent while he did so.

Jim remembered his schooldays and the description of the Maide Eamainn, the stick the Old Irish used to secure their wattle doors against the wind. All in all, if he was to attempt an escape, this was not a step in the right direction.

The daily confession had taken on a more serious, and sinister direction. This poor sinner, as his abductor now called himself, was revealing more of the soul stains he needed forgiveness for.

At the beginning, in what was the first confession, Jim heard him say that he had abducted other people, several times. He reasoned that they might still be around the house, in other confinements, on other rail lines. This thought had given him some comfort that there might be a way out for him and the others. Now the matter of fact voice had jolted him into a new and terrible reality; the way out for these others had been death.

"The first one, her name was Paula, Paula Stafford, initials PS on the tree. I tried to get her to stay, make her stay, but she was headstrong. I wanted her as a companion for me and for Grammy. I wanted a female companion and not to be alone. When she would not stay, I made sure she would stay. She is down in the wood now waiting for me. I know she will come back. For these and all of the sins of my past life I'm sorry. Am I absolved?"

From the first words Jim's mind was racing. *I knew there was more to this than getting drunk or using swear words. Now we are getting down to the nitty gritty; but how am I going to handle this so that I can get some kind of advantage or have him depend on me for longer. When he gets to the end of these confessions he will probably bump me off and capture another priest to hear that confession. This guy would probably want a Bishop or a Cardinal to hear that one.*

"Did you harm the girl, my son?" He knew the answer. *Think, think, you have to string this out until you get some idea of how to react.*

"Only when she would not stay"

"Did you plan it? Did you consciously plan to…"
murder No! Not murder, careful, slow, "force her to stay."

"No."

"So it was spur of the moment."

"Yes"

Take another tack. Keep this going. "Did you offend against the Sixth Commandment my son?"

Georgie was stunned. This was not going the way he imagined. Fanahans leering face came quickly into his mind. The pub conversation on confession. He could hear the whinging voice, Ridein' women, ridein' women. Gettin' your hole. Laying pipe. Givin' her one. Cleaning yer pipes.

He roared. He jumped up and kicked the side of the box. He kicked the door. He was suffocating. He needed to be out. He needed Grammy, to hold him, to console him, to comfort him. He kicked open the door and stumbled out of the box.

Jim felt the outburst before he heard it. Something in his simple question had caused a volcano to erupt. The box shook with the violence. He heard the door bang open and heard the footsteps fading.

He looked up at his door. Nice one Jim. *The bloody stick is still in place. Shit? I'm stuck.*

There was no candlelight dinner for Jim that night. Cramped and in need of a toilet he sat and waited.

When after several uncomfortable hours he heard the stick being withdrawn, his bursting bladder and the pain, ensured that his captor was long departed, before he crawled out of the box, and along the landing, back to his quarters.

Chapter 15

Precision and order were the cornerstone of Georgie's life. Each day had its own routine: the routine was the key, and normality, he believed, had been the lock that kept his secrets.

Each weekday he rose at half past six, had his toast and tea and using the remainder of the hot water left in the kettle, shaved and washed. As he completed his toilet, a second kettle was boiling, this was used to prepared breakfast for the priest.

He kept the teapot warm with a tea cosy and placed it, the toast, and the marmalade in the dining room. Carefully, quietly, he released the lock on the priest's room, let himself out, and walked the mile to the station: to catch the eight o'clock train to the city.

At a quarter past nine o'clock he was in the business ready to direct the events of the day. He remained working in his office when the staff went out to lunch, in whatever Bistro or Pub was the current fashionable place.

Exactly at a quarter to five he left the office, instructing his office manager to close up. He walked to the station to catch the five fifteen to Port. Each evening he arrived home just in time for the evening evnts.

For the past number of days now it was a cleansing confession.

On Friday, he left the office early so that he could have an end of duty drink, in Milo's.

On Saturdays he rose at seven, and having completed the normal morning chores, went out into the town to select the groceries. Precisely at three o'clock these would be delivered to him at the gates of his estate.

On Saturday and Sunday afternoon, he walked the short distance to the Commercial Hotel for two large brandies, and to receive good wishes from those townspeople who still remembered the family, and their stature in the town.

Each day and week he would follow this routine, and in this routine was the key, and normality – the lock that, up to now, had kept all his secrets – especially the big ones.

But it was not always like that. Was it Mumsie?

When Eithne Bowen discovered she was pregnant she didn't know how she would tell The Duchess or The Major. It was bad enough being pregnant; being pregnant by one of the farm workers was an added inconvenience. No! It was more than an inconvenience: it was a catastrophe

She knew when she started seeing Solomon Smith, the son of the Woodsman, that the family would see it as wrong. They would have wanted her to wait, and be courted by a son of one of the eligible families in the town; or from one of the nearby country estates.

At eighteen years of age she was fed up waiting. She was a young woman who needed romance. She needed to experience the world and the joys and fruits therein.

The Major always said she was self-willed. Her formal education was now complete, her tutors had departed. For the first time in her life she was her own woman; with no one to tell her what to do, or how to behave, or where to take her pleasures and fun.

It was that fun and pleasure of a night under the stars,

when she had seduced Solomon, that now left her in her present condition.

The Duchess arranged for her to go away. The Major never knew the story, until she returned a year later, with the baby. He ranted, and he raved, and kicked his hunter around the estate, the town, and the countryside.

In the three weeks he took to purge his rage and anger he rode over a few flimsy animal shelters, rode up a lot of the harvested fields, and knocked over a peasant or two, but with no serious injury, or any serious damage: to his own crops or property.

In the end he returned. "Keep your bastard out of my sight. Keep to your own part of the house."

The Duchess helped her to raise George. She kept appeasing The Major, and in the end a cease-fire was declared. As long as she kept George out of the way the uneasy peace prevailed.

The two women took over the rearing of the baby, looked after his needs, educated him and when he was disobedient, took care of his punishment themselves.

Whenever The Major referred to him, complained about him, or blamed him for some incident, he called him The Bastard.

It was only in old age, in his forgetfulness, that he began referring to George as The Boy. Just before he died he referred to him, once only, as George Edward Bowen, my grandson: although there was no other issue in the family he didn't say – and heir.

Chapter 16

Bob Tyrell walked the ten minutes to work each morning. He did it for exercise. He did it to meet the other members of the community who were out and about early. He did it so that people who might like to bump-in to him, outside of the office – the police station, could do so if necessary. Over the years his morning walks had been very productive in obtaining information and tips.

The Monday morning after the abduction he hurried more that usual. Acknowledging greetings, but continuing to walk, just waving and smiling, when someone tried to engage him in conversation.

He was eager to see if the weekend investigations had produced any results. Fanahan and his team would have been out beating the bushes in most of the pubs, night clubs and even alleyways of the city.

It was odds-on Bob thought, that the kidnapper was a new player in the crime game, and not any of the existing crime bosses, or terrorist leaders who frequently pulled abductions for profit, or to keep control over their drug markets.

As he read the reports he realized his hunch was probably true, no clues left at the scene, no usable fingerprints, no information from informers, no one could put anyone in the frame.

He read on ... 'it was practically the end of the confession hour - just a few ladies in the church - no one noticed anything of much use.'

He frowned at Fanahan's report, as he noticed the usual ironic style in the statement, 'and the blind woman, and her dog, of course could tell us nothing.'

Tyrell wondered if the blind woman could have been Aoife. It was her church too. It made sense and the dog, her Guide dog, Sheba.

The chimes of the door bell had barely faded when Aoife asked from inside the door, "Who's there please?"

"Aoife. It's Bob Tyrell. How are you?"

Aoife opened the door on the chain. "Superintendent Tyrell, it's good to see you. How are all the family?"

"Good Aoife, good, in the best of health. Hello Sheba" he said, as Sheba checked him out.

Satisfied Aoife opened the door fully. "Come on in Bob, I'll make us a cup of tea."

As the tea, scones and marmalade were being laid out strategically, so that Aoife could serve them as simply as possible, Bob explained the purpose of his visit.

"Yes, Bob. I was there at the time. I don't expect I can be of much help to you. I noticed very little."

She reviewed her thoughts for a while, playing the incident over again in her mind. "I was kind of engrossed in my own thoughts. God forgive me, I'm in the church, I was supposed to be praying but I'm wondering: what will I get for the dinner. I heard him open the confession box. He asked Father Jim to get out. An accident he said, but that's all. I just heard their hurrying footsteps as they rushed out. It's amazing that people whisper in a church; but they can still be heard all over the place."

Aoife and Bob were at the end of the tea and scones and the conversation. He was disappointed. He wasn't sure what he had expected but he had hoped for more, a word, a smell remembered by Aoife, an impression, something to make progress in the case.

"Aoife, that's fine, that's a pity. I was hoping you noticed something heard something. I was hoping – that's all. I'll see you Aoife. Bye Sheba." He bent to pat Sheba, and rub vigorously between her front legs, on her chest.

He patted Aoife on the arm, and turned to leave, when she added softly as if thinking out loud. "Perhaps The Quiet Man, as Sheba and myself call him, upstairs in the balcony saw something."

Confessions were almost ended when Frank noticed the stranger enter the church aisle beneath him. He seemed unsure of where he was going and turned to collided with the blind lady, as she moved out of the seat, where she normally sat with her dog.

He reached the altar and genuflected. Frank was surprised to notice that he wore a pair of handmade brown brogue shoes. Unusual, nowadays he thought, handmade shoes, they even have a crest or something like it, on the instep.

Noticing the handmade shoes was natural for Frank. Masie and himself laughed at his hobby, of trying to predict what a customer who came into The Drapery, might buy.

Frank always said, if a man wearing a well-tailored handmade suit, with a matching handmade shirt and hand crafted shoes came into their shop: he was there looking for directions to somewhere else.

Bob was well pleased with his mornings work. Himself, Aoife and of course Sheba had tracked Frank down in the quietness of the church gallery.

They had talked over coffee in the Coffee Dock, in one of the new giant shopping centres, now populating the city suburbs.

Afterwards Aoife decided to make her own way home. Bob watched her – amazed as he always was, by the grace and confidence of her progress through the busy, and noisy streets.

Sheba is some guide dog, he thought, always very intent in getting to where, she has been instructed to lead.

He was very surprised, when Sheba seemed to stop her forward progress, to stand and growl at a passing pedestrian. Her sudden halt, surprised Aoife and caused her to stumble.

"No voice Sheba. Quiet." It was all over in a moment. *That's very unusual for Sheba. I must ask Aoife if she knows what all that was about.*

An hour later, Bob reviewed his notes and transcribed the bullet points onto the white board in his office.

"Now" he said, as he stood back to see where this might lead him. "As Missus Beeton says. To make rabbit stew, first catch the rabbit. I wonder, how many people in the country make bespoke shoes?"

Chapter 17

Fanahan was starting to hate this pub. It brought back un-happy memories. That Hoor Tyrell and his leads. Who else would go and ask a blind auld bag what she saw, when the priest was kidnapped. Who would think that an auld piss-pot up in the Church gallery, would come up with a clue that had caused him so much grief. Handmade bloody shoes, now Tyrell would have them all off chasing the bloody shoe clue down, and he had his bollix chewed off for not turning it up: in first place.

"And the blind woman, and her dog, of course could tell us nothing." Tyrell had read it out loud at the briefing not once, or twice but three times.

"Jaysus Shay! Did you even interview the woman?"

The shagger' went on to cover his interview with the bag and the piss-pot, and when Fanahan thought it was all over concluded with.

"And the blind woman, and her dog, of course could tell us nothing. Cross of Christ" he roared. "I wish all witnesses were as observant."

Now to cap it all, Milo that Meath bastard, had put the framed photos back on the pub walls.

There it was in full view: in front of him. **Cavan All Ireland Football Champions.** Shite! And next to it, **Galway All Ireland Football - Beaten Finalists**.

Milo had obviously heard of his balls-up, or he would never be so brave, as to drag out the photos again. *Feck him. He's trying to rub this in again.*

"Moynalty is nearly in Cavan" he squealed, each time Fanahan complained. "I'll adorn me pub as I want."

One of these days I'll feckin' adorn you with a split feckin' head!

He could see it all again. Galway had played it well and now they had just scored a point, with only minutes to go. It was Galway 2 Goals and 13 Points to Cavan's 18 Points – translated for the foreigners tuning-in all over the World – Galway 19. Cavan 18. He was looking at his watch and roaring "Blow the feckin' whistle – REF!"

"Easy, easy – take your time." He advised the Cavan goalkeeper, as he prepared to kick the ball out, and restart play. "Put it into the stands" he roared. It was a long straight kick: into midfield.

Now, and as when it had happened for the first time: years ago. He viewed the action – in slow motion.

The ball came dropping down and with a leap that would rival, the Kerry maestro Micko, collecting a ball at midfield, Tyrell reached high and cleanly caught it. He landed, took one step sideways, to avoid a tackle, then shot high and accurately over the crossbar. The stadium erupted with Cavan voices.

The commentator sang "And once again the sides are level." A bloody replay. We'll slaughter you in the bloody replay, Fanahan thought.

The Galway keeper wasn't thinking of a replay, as he quickly retrieved the ball, and blasted a long kick up towards his half forward line. "One of you shaggers kick a point" he roared.

The ball was dropping down, well up-field near the Cavan end, when Fanahan saw Tyrell.

He was racing back from his midfield position, into the Galway forward line. He shouldered players out of his way and once again leaped skywards. Fanahan looked at the referee. He was looking at his watch and raising the whistle to his lips. "To late Tyrell" Fanahan shouted. "To bloody late."

Tyrell collected the ball: landed, and looked towards the Galway goal. He hopped the ball once, as if he had all the time in the world, then blasted it towards the goal. The referee had the whistle to his mouth as he heard all of the stadium erupt. Cavan voices roaring "Go on, ya boy, ya." Galway voices howling "Blow the whistle REF."

The referee hesitated, and looked high, at the ball drifting overhead. He took the whistle from his lips and watched as the ball went straight and true between the posts. When the ball hit the netting behind the goal: he blew full time.

On radio sets all over the World, from America to Australia, the score was given: Cavan 20 points, Galway 19 Points.

Feck him - Fanahan thought. Feck him for then. And Feck him for this week.

"Milo!" He thundered. "Get those feckin' pictures off the walls – I won't be back 'till you do."

Feck you – thought Milo, as he softly said, "Gotcha" and punched his fist into the air.

Cl.

Bob Tyrell checked his bullet ¡
clues, and noted, that apart fror
days, they now knew: that to ma
handmade shoe service, in Irelan
Provence of Leinster, was going
for the foot soldiers.

Another figure on his white b   ᴗᴗused him
considerable worry. In Ireland over the last ten years there
were almost one hundred people who had disappeared
without trace. Some of these he knew would be runaways, of
all ages, who for one reason or another left home: intending
to lose themselves.

There were also thirty-five people, in the province, who
were believed to have been abducted and who seemingly
disappeared without trace.

It's a lot, Bob thought. A lot of families waiting and
wondering! Out loud he said to himself. "To bloody many!
What are we missing here?"

With that idea foremost in his mind he picked up the list
of cobblers, fancy cobblers, he thought as he looked down
the names. *The drive to Kildare might settle the old
reasoning juices. Hello Mister, or Missus Prunty of Prunty's
Made to Measure Footwear Emporium Kildare. I'm on me
way.*

Walking to his car in the Garda station car park he
noticed, perhaps for the first time in over a week, that it was
turning into a season of mild, sunny days. *Won't be long
now 'till I might get a days fishing on the lakes.*

Prunty's Made to Measure Footwear

small annex behind a larger Saddle, Harness
Shop that probably had a good trade and wealthy
mers, because it was beside the Curragh Racecourse,
d the nearby racehorse training establishments.

Junior Prunty explained. "Racing is, 'The Sport of
Kings'. These boyos don't wear crowns on their heads, but
they do wear mass produced shoes on their feet. Most-times
the horses are better shod than some of these bucks, what
with syndicates, and clubs owning horseflesh these days. We
diversified and went for, where the market is, that's the
horses themselves. Haven't done a handmade for a long
time. In fact, I never did any at all. That was the father and
he's well-on in age, and only comes in now and then to do
the odd repair for his old customers, or to help me pick out
good quality leather. A great man for knowing quality he is.
You know the only problem he had with the shoes – was
that they wouldn't wear out. No redundant parts there."
Hearing a footfall he looked around. "God almighty, it's
better be born lucky than rich! There he is now. He said he
might come in today, to put a brad in a pair of his own."

Senior Prunty was small, as thin as a rail and eighty years
old: if he was a day. Bob followed him, around and into the
dark, tanned leather perfumed interior, of the Emporium. It
was a large one room shop, with a circular area of work
benches, and an inevitable collection of not finished, half
finished, and waiting for collection shoes: cluttering the
shelves on the walls.

"I only do the odd bit Sir" Senior explained. "Most of the owners of these shoes will never need them any more, up in the graveyard, where they are now. I had a fellow once left in a pair for heels, and went off foreign to work for five years. He came in when he came back, and handed me the docket. It took me an hour to find his shoes. Come back next week, says I to him. They'll be ready then."

Cackling and laughing, spluttering and muttering, "Ready next week" he asked, "What can I do for you?"

Bob briefly told of the investigation underway, and how Frank had come to the opinion that the kidnapper was wearing handmade shoes, and he was just following that lead.

Senior was sorry but they had not made many pairs in the last few years, "But you know" he said. "Mine lasted for years. Twenty sometimes and if they were looked after and kept well, they could last a lifetime. I know some auld customers who left their shoes to their sons, in their will. No they didn't. I just like the story."

"Have you a customer list? Bob asked, pretty sure that what ever he got would be useless, and a cold trail.

"I keep that with the lasts. It could take a while."

"The lasts?"

"The forms. The shapes, the dummy feet. We took measurements and made a wooden copy of the foot and used that with a bottom – as a form to make the shoes on. I have all of these stored somewhere at the back here. I can make a list but it will take a while. It could take a good while. It will be ready next week" Senior cackled. "No, I'm only joking. Could you come back in an hour, or so?"

"I'm on a tight schedule. When you have it, can you drop it into the local Garda station – ask them to send it up to me in Dublin. They'll know where to send it. Thanks."

Chapter 19

Life, Detective Fanahan decided, was not treating him well. He was working hard collecting and making out lists of wankers who were rich enough to afford handmade shoes.

He had been pulled off his usual streets and was travelling all over the city and county visiting cobblers who made the stupid things. When you look at it, it was probably the right decision, he decided since none of his usual sources had provided him with any useful information.

Nowadays the number of people who ordered handmade shoes was small, and the customer names held by the cobblers, were old and outdated. He had searched the phone book for several but found that either they were no longer listed, or when he did get a name and rang through he found they were deceased .

To top it all – he was missing his local pub. He couldn't go back to the feckin' Meath Man's after storming out.

As far as he could find out the bloody pictures were still hanging on the walls.

Being out and about in parts of the town where he was not well known had advantages, a nice pint at lunchtime being one of them, another was that expense for daytime meals consumed away from base, did not need receipts.

He parked the car outside his next call: Bootery for the Uppers. It was garish, bright, and beside a rundown boarded-up out-of-business sexy-underwear shop called One for Everybody in the Audience.

I bet it would still be open if they had called it Knickers for Nobs. My humour is improving. I think , I'll give Milo another chance later-on. I wonder will I boot open the door of the Bootery . He pushed the door open, but didn't enter. "Helloo. Anybody hooo-me?"

He approached his task, without any other thought on his mind, than to check if they had a list of the customers who bought handmade from them. When he entered the shop he was surprised to see it was run-down, dusty, and not as well stocked as he had imagined.

Three people were in the shop, they were moving to leave, through a back entrance. One of them, the spotty teenager with a stud in her nose, a line of hoops in her ear, and spiky red hair, came back towards him.

"Ya want sum-min?"

Fanahan had seen those eyes before, heard that snarl before, saw that pallor before.

He lowered his voice. "Is this Bootery for the Uppers?" He asked, with the emphasis on – the uppers.

"Uppers. Yea. Ya want sum-min"

"Where are they?" He asked looking around at the dusty shelves.

"Wha?"

"The boots?"

"Wha' boots?" She asked slowly following his gaze.

"The ones you sell!" He prompted.

"Don't."

Suddenly getting with the cover story she said. "They're gone. Moo-ved. Last year."

Ignoring her Fanahan said. "I want a pair for horseridin'." Pointedly: he repeated the word. "Ridin. You know." He motioned holding a reins with his hands, and pushed his hips forward, back again, then forward.

Innocently: he continued. "Horse?"

"Wha?" She mouthed again as these familiar words, in an unfamiliar setting, reached her brain.

"A pair of boots?"

"Gone." She said again. "Moved." This time the word came out more distinctly.

"Where?" Noticing the stare become blanker he added. "Where did they move to? Did they leave a forwarding address?"

"No dresses either." She said. "No more. Gone. Moved, years ago."

"What do you sell? Here."

"Nuttin'. Don't it's storage."

"What kind of storage?"

"Things. Just things. Stuff like."

The door at the back of the shop opened. A youth, perhaps no older than eighteen or nineteen, came quickly down the shop floor.

"What can I do for you, Pal? You." He said turning on the girl. "You're wanted. Back there."

"Wha', Where? Who wan's me?"

"Get back there!" He said, and pushed the girl towards the swinging, slowly closing door.

Fanahan moved, trying to see what was behind the door. A smeared plasterboard wall, with a faded map of Dublin City, was quickly covered as the man stood before him and asked again. "Who are ya lookin' for?"

"Just some information on The Bootery."

"Gone. Moved. Not here any more - went outa business."

"OK. Thanks. Sorry for troubling you." Fanahan moved to turn towards the door.

The youth had also turned, now he sensed that Fanahan was watching him. He stopped, turning his head, but not his body, over his shoulder, he said, "Yeah. Ya gone yet?"

"I'm gone." Fanahan replied. *But not forgotten. Not forgotten, Anto.*

Anto entered the back room where the mules had delivered the consignments that were now being broken down for delivery. He called the girl to him, then struck her hard across the face: she recoiled. He raised his foot and slammed his sole into her mid-drift.

She fell and sprawled onto the floor. "He's a fecking copper. Yous lot get a move on. Get this bleedin' stuff packed and outa here. Now. I'm calling The Boss."

He turned, hoping that no one noticed he was in a big hurry. He opened the back door to the alley, checked left, looked right, he moved out, squinting in the glare, checking the flat garage roofs of the houses behind. His heart pounding, he ran, hoping the end of the alleyway, was still clear.

Fanahan sat in the car talking on his mobile. "Get here as fast as you can. Bring your lads: ones you trust. I think it's a depot, a drug distribution centre."

The fishwife, dressed and hidden by her shawl, moved into the alley. Her long smelly barrow, squeaked on a loose wheel. She did not acknowledge, the shouted warnings from the lads, and the girl, who scampered past.

By the time the heavy gang of Gardaí reached the Bootery, Watcher had emptied it of the drug consignment and was on the phone to the boss.

On Friday, back in Milo's, Shay admired his settling pint and The Evening Herald headline.

DRUGS BUST and under this, Distribution Centre Raided.

Again he read the article. It made the operation look good. It wasn't however, by the time the lads got there the place was empty. The crew was left in the shits – called out on a Wild Goose Chase. He had to leak the story – his story, to keep the management off their backs.

I'll get you next time, Anto.

He raised his pint, tilted the glass and moved it forward.

He nodded at Milo. "Thank you Milo. I'll have another welcome back round."

Gotcha.

Chapter 20

Bob Tyrell was despondent as time passed and no progress was made in the case of the kidnapped priest. Despite the constant pressure from the Church it was now only getting sporadic mention in the newspapers.

He had glanced at the headlines of the papers in the public office this morning and learned that some county footballers had shown their arses in a hotel, and that a prisoner on day release came back to the prison alone because the warders with him got delayed in a fracas in a pub.

He was considering putting the kidnap case on a low priority. It looked like all the work done to assemble list of people who had ordered handmade shoes was a waste. The lists were long, outdated and a devil to work on since most of them were hand written: badly hand written at that.

Verifying these list was taking so much time in cross-checking with telephone directories and voter's list or business directories. For every one current trading name: there was five that were not.

This is going to get us nowhere, even if it's the only real lead we have. What we need is a break, some new evidence, someone who saw something and has not come forward yet.

It's a shame that we don't even have enough details to mount a public appeal. We could appeal for more eye witnesses, but since it all happened in the church area we have those.

We don't even have a consistent description of the vehicle that might mean we can appeal for anyone who saw it. All in all we don't have much. He fingered through the day's post and other papers on his desk.

Because of the elaborate handwriting copperplate style: one neatly bound sheaf of papers caught his attention. He lifted it out and recognized what it was. I should have expected something like this, he thought as the top page came into view. It's Pruntys list. The top page was a letter addressed to him.

Dear Bob,

Since at my age most people I meet, converse with, or communicate with are younger that me, forgive me the familiarity of using your Christian Name in address.

I enclose some pages of information on my customers whom I know are still, like me thank God, in this land of the living. Unfortunately, it comes to only forty-two names.

Forgive me also for giving you extra work. To expedite delivery I have sent you the original pages. I would appreciate their return when you have made copies. They contain some personal comments or notes – I made at the time. I hope that you can extract the details you need without much trouble and that an old man ramblings will not distract you.

I wish you every success with the case and remain sincerely yours,

Stephen Prunty Snr.

Bob untied the bundle. They were yellow cards about as long as a normal page, but a little narrower. Each had two holes punched on the left margin.

He reasoned they had been kept in file folders, and because of a decent system of records had been fairly near to hand and not to hard to find.

I wish they all had your organization Senior he prayed as he remembered some of the other lists he had seen or heard comments on from his team.

Some of them even had what the lads were now calling "MD's" in their reports. "Opened shoe box - 36 pages of names and 42 MD's".

He knew it was a rib directed at him, and he was fairly sure it would have originated with Fanahan.

Counting and recording mouse droppings, after the criticism of how he missed the information which Aoife and her guide dog Sheba provided, would be just the kind of puerile action that would appeal to him.

Bob took a long sip from his morning cup of tea, dunked a Rich Tea biscuit and started to read the first record.

Customer Name:
John Flynn, Cloncrave, Co. Westmeath.
This was followed by specific measurements of all parts of his foot: toes, heel, instep, length, width and a traced drawing of his sole. There was even some comments about Mister Flynn's weight distribution and how the shoe assembler, for that was what Senior called him, should proceed.

Assembler Note - Due to his weight and height, he wears his shoes badly (as he tends to throw his shoulders back, as he walks). In orders for this customer: re-enforce the heel and if possible add a slight uplift to the back insole of the shoe.

Underneath in the comment's portion of the page – Mr. Flynn pays on time and is the third member of his family to come to us for service. He has also through his business sent us several referrals who like himself are type A customers.

What followed "A,17,9,U,4,Sunny", had Bob wondering but he could make some of it out. The A he thought probably was for A customer status. The 17, 9 and 4 since they had their lower numbers ready crossed out were some kind of running totals.

As for the rest he had no idea and no clue to what they might mean. It was unlikely to be important to his investigation.

If he remembered, he would ask Senior when he returned the lists. *This time I'm definitely going to bring a fishing rod.*

Bob flicked quickly through the remaining sheets. Reading some, but not really taking much of the information in: his unconscious mind was already starting to wind down the case. This information will take a lot of time, to check, and follow up.

He drained his remaining cold tea and threw the bundle onto the middle of his desk. The pages bounced softly, skidded off the shiny cover of the Garda News for May, and fluttered off onto the floor.

Bob moved to the front of his office and carefully picked them up. *If I'm lucky they fell in bundles and I can get these back in order quickly.*

His hopes fell. Some of the records, obeying a gravity he had not accounted for, fell out of the middle of the pile, and scattered on the floor again.

He picked them up and tried to shuffle them back into card-deck symmetry. He read the uppermost page: where did

this fall out of, he wondered, as he read the three lines of
Seniors copperplate hand.

Despite my best attempts I can't take to this man. He
has a surly manner and if it wasn't for the family I would
send him packing.
He reminds me of a man I once knew who was a secret
dog kicker.

The other side of the page was blank. He re-arranged
the remaining papers.
None of this has been any good, lists, lists, names, no
clues – no bloody help – a lot of work and no progress at
all. I might as well throw it all out.
But instead, he placed the papers in several manilla file
covers. He. secured them together with several elastic bands:
big, thick, strong bands, and placed them in his out-tray with
the note. FILE - Abduction Jim Gaffney.
He remembered those that were Prunty's cards! *He
wanted them back.*
He undid the elastic, reached into the files and called
the Desk Sergeant. "Can you make copies of these, please,"
he said, "and leave them back on my desk."
I'll run down with them tomorrow, he thought.
Blast, his mind added, as almost in a daze from far away, he
watched the wind bend and shake the car park trees, blowing
pink cherry blossom flowers, across the tarmac.
*No fishing in that wind. but, I'll still throw a rod in the
boot just in case it dies down, Waders too, and later... I'll sit
down and pick some flies.* He started to tidy his desk again.
That's it, that's what we have! After all the work... that's it.
Without waiting for an answer he continued, now

talking out-loud to himself. "When I was a rookie and worked on a case like this – what did I do?"

He went back to his silent thinking. *It seems long ago, usually I would plough through reams of paper. Sometimes you have the forensic evidence.*

Deep down now within his mind, thinking in a daydream, he took off his coat, threw it on a chair, sat at his desk and loosened his tie.

Memories of Cavan on a Sunday morning ran through his dream.

First thing home after Mass was to get out of the tight things into more comfortable, more often-worn clothes, work clothes, no time to rest even on the Sabbath: cows don't know it's Sunday.

He sat still, returning to his internal commentary, telling himself, in silent words, things his mind already knew. But it wasn't just that: it was an evaluation of the evidence stepped out, and examined for clarity.

No one saw anything. Or if they did it was all too familiar. Nothing looked out of place. A priest in a church. Just the shoes. Keep looking; there is more in here. I've been over all of that several times. I can't see anything; if there's anything there we all missed it. Something that looks fine: but is out of place; like it was out of step, with what was going on around it.

Aoife is in the church and only becomes aware of what happened: almost as it is over.

But Frank Gowan says that the kidnapper and Aoife bumped into one another.

How did she miss that? Did we miss that also? She bumped into him. Cross of Christ! I think he bumped into her: an every day happening for a blind woman, bumps;

81

consigned to her subconscious, almost as soon as it happened. Gowan says collide. He says: they collided. What caused that?

Where was the dog? Did he fall over the dog? I've done that many times. Mine gets under my feet all the time. Did she move out? And did the kidnapper fall over the dog and grab her for support? Not a guide dog! The dog would have avoided him, kept her safe.

In the back of his mind another scene replayed itself. Aoife walking down the street and Sheba turning to look at a passer-by. Aoife almost stumbling over the dog.

"I wonder. Does this fellow like dogs? More to the point do dogs like him?"

He remembered a cackling voice, heard that cackling voice say ready next week and saw hand written copperplate words "a secret dog kicker".

"Hey! Shit I'm slipping. This case may not be as dead as we thought. No! It is! I'm clutching at straws. It couldn't be that simple."

The Desk Sergeant returned with the copies and was bemused to hear his Super mutter, "Corny as it may seem, I think I need to go and see a dog about a man."

Chapter 21

"I just remember someone bumping into me a while before I heard Father Jim walk out of the box. I didn't think it could be him, the kidnapper, though. Do you want more tea, Bob?"

"No Aoife, this is fine. Frank Gowan said in his evidence that the kidnapper bumped into you on his way up the church. I'm wondering did he fall over the dog?"

Bob placed his cup and saucer on the table: well in from the edge, where later Aoife could collect it with least trouble.

"It would be unusual Bob for anyone to fall over Sheba, she is very good like that. She is trained to avoid occasions that could be a danger for me. It would be very unusual."

Bob noticed the frown on her face, the confusion. He knew she was going back over the occasion in her mind. She shook her head slowly.

Maybe if I change the subject for a while she might remember something. "When you left Frank and myself the day we met, as you walked away, Sheba stopped and blocked your progress up the path. Did she sense some danger perhaps? Or was it just something odd that occurred?"

Aoife said very quickly. "It was that man again I suspect, the one I believe kicked her or still kicks her when he gets the opportunity. It's hard to believe people like that can be so cruel to animals."

Cackle, cackle, in Bobs mind. A man who kicks dogs. "Why do they do it Aoife?"

"They don't like dogs I think they are afraid of them and kick them to make sure they stay away and don't bite them. I don't know for sure, perhaps they were once bitten."

"And," Bob continued. "Does someone kick her?"

"Someone has kicked her before. She cries in pain, but always, up to lately anyhow, continued with her job. It took me a while to work it out. I thought she was walking on something that hurt her foot, or her leg. When I came home I checked her out but she was all right. One day I felt her sides, and she whined in pain. So, I think someone kicked her. She growls now: when she sees him. I feel it's a man."

"It was a man, I think she knew it was him in the street." Bob offered as he bent to pat and rub Sheba, and spoke softly to console her.

"Was it a bad man Sheba? Did he kick you? Don't worry I'm looking for him now and with a bit of luck I'll catch him and put him where he can't hurt you."

He stood up and reached out to touch Aoife on the arm. "I think it's the same man, I think she startled him in the church. That's why he bumped into you. He was trying to get away from her. I think he's really scared of her now that she is growling at him. If you don't mind I would like you to walk along that street for a few days, around the same time, I'll have a plain clothes man watching you. If Sheba growls we will move in. God knows it's a long shot, but it's all we have to go on so far."

Chapter 22

Bob and Senior Prunty sat in the morning sun outside The Emporium and after the small-talk and the weather-talk was out of the way they came to the purpose of Bob's visit: men who kick dogs.

"It amuses me. They'll go up to the Elephant in the Zoo and hold out food for him to take with his trunk. They'll stand where a fired up stallion, going down to the start at the Curragh, will prance and snort, and kick the rails as he passes them; but put them in a ten acre field with a little terrier and they go to pieces." Prunty Senior was in full flow, "And what's their answer? Kick the beejapers outa poor dogs. The quieter the better."

Bob took out a single page – the orphan dropped on the floor page, of the customer list and passed it over to Senior. "Can you remember who you wrote this about?" He asked as Senior adjusted his glasses and read his three statements.

"Don't even have to look it up. It's Bowen, George E. Bowen. Family's from Port Siney His grandfather and the granny, Duchess we used call her, were decant folk, young George is a pup! When he came to me: I would have sent him packing if it wasn't for the family. He only got two pair from me at any rate, paid for the first lot and kicked up a row about the second pair. Said they were pinching him. Aye! Pinching his pocket most likely. I think the price became a problem. I felt that we were well shut of him, so I left the shoes with him as an inducement to go. I sent him a bill after. I knew he wouldn't pay, but I knew too it would keep him away from the place. If he ever came back: he knew the first thing I would do was ask for the money. It worked! I haven't seen him in an age."

Bob was quickly scanning the other pages in the bundle, balanced on his knee, he found what he was looking for.

Customer Name:

George E. Bowen, Bowen Court, Port Siney.

Z,9,2,G,0,Bwsy.

He gave it to Senior and asked "What's the code mean?"

Senior cackled, "Ah that! Just a quick way of knowing who I'm dealing with. In the case of George it means that he had no customer rating when I wrote that. His family were always good customers, prompt payers. George had just got the one pair at the time. I had done nine pairs for the family, his grandfather introduced him to us and George had so far introduced no one else to us and the rest, Ah well, that's just me. I thought he was a Bowsey."

Changing tack, as if serious talk and remembering was making him to melancholy he cackled again and said. "Did I ever tell you about the one legged man that when he first came to me, only wanted one complete shoe, a left one. He asked for another shoe top, tongue, lace holes, laces and all, without a sole - to put on the bottom of the wooden leg? No! Well I'll tell you all about it. We need a good cheer up and a laugh. It's what keeps me going - a good yarn and a laugh and I'll give you a conundrum to work on. Every other time he came to me he bought a pair of shoes. How was that?"

He cackled and repeated 'A pair of shoes and him with only one leg! Work that one out."

It was a good yarn and a good laugh Bob reflected as he started the car, a pair of shoes, two left shoes one for now and one for later. He rang the Chief and it was a good day he decided, as he crossed the Curragh and relayed the news. "The kidnapper of the priest, I have a suspect, a name. I think we found our man."

"Yes I have an address."

"No Chief, we better hold of on the raid. Just in case Father Gaffney, is not in the house and we tip yer man off. It's to soon. So it is. I'm on the way back to the shop. I should be there in thirty to forty minutes. Can you ask the lads in the shop in Port Siney, to give us all they know about George E. Bowen from Bowen Court."

Tyrell had his man: he was sure of it: all the clues pointed to Bowen. The shoes, the fear of the dog and the fact that the dog seemed to sense it. The location. Jesus! Port Siney.

He moved the car at speed into the inside Dublin bound lane of the Motorway, carefully watching a large truck speeding by in the overtaking lane with it's convey of smaller cars cruising to close behind: in the slipstream.

Suddenly the third car in the truck parade, dived into the lane in front of him and began an undertaking attack. The truck driver noticing the move in his inside wing mirror, slowly moved in and closed the gap, forcing the undertaking driver, and Bob to brake sharply.

Bob cursed, wound down the window, and reached down – searching below his seat. He found what he wanted, and placed the magnetically attached, siren lamp, above his door and switched it on.

Within seconds the road ahead was clear as he blue-flashed and siren wailed his way ahead.

Chapter 23

When O'Neill first worked with Traonach – The Invisible Corncrake, he needed a good inconspicuous lookout to help him plan IRA raids and the more important get-away routes.

When Shane set up the drugs operation he knew that with him exiled to Amsterdam he needed a good reliable, blend in, don't be noticed pair of eyes, to watch out for him in Ireland.

Traonach took the job, and in the past few years this decision to bring him on board had proved a wise one.

Police raids were often anticipated, minor and major revolts, and their ringleaders, were quickly stamped out: before they really began. His enemies, within and outside the operation knew he had eyes and ears somewhere, but they never found out where.

Back in Dublin Traonach met him and brought him up to date. Anto and the girl were at her flat, if it was a normal night, by ten o'clock she would be out of her head, juiced to the gills. He would be out to strut his stuff in the late night bars and clubs. A little drink, a little talk, a little deal under the table and a little more money, for the Anto Nixer Fund.

O'Neill decided Traonach would pick up the girl around midnight, stash her in the boot of the car and they would pick up Anto a little later.

He examined the bag, it contained, a heavy lump hammer and a nice long, thin shiny, ten inch narrow spike.

This time Anto I am going to crucify you by one hand only, I still need you alive and wounded as an example.

Thud! Thud! The hammer hit the spike and it went further through his wrist and into the wooden railway sleeper. Anto screamed loudly and O'Neill said "No one to hear Anto! Sticky fingers Anto? Sticky with blood this time not my dope. You robbed me. You put a consignment at risk by running away:"

This was a good trip the girl decided, better than the usual buzz, as she looked on with both horror and fascination.

Horror, that Anto was getting this punishment for just feckin' a few grams of dope, and fascination at the scene before her.

Anto screaming and struggling on his back on the railway sleeper: between the tracks, crucified by that one spike through his left wrist, his legs trashing and banging on the gravel, his free arm trying to push the big man off, as each blow drove the spike deeper into the wood and broke his tendons, burst his veins and scraped his bones.

Her shouts and her moans, at the orgasm crashing through her, were drowned out by his screams and the crash of the hammer blows.

She had come before when Anto hit her a dig as he came and she cried dig me again, dig me again Anto, harder, harder, again. But never crashing, spasms like this. The next one not waiting for the previous one to finish, on and on, damp, and breath taking and knee trembling.

Wave after wave, pounding on, as the blood spurted and Anto groaned and the sweat, she was sure it would be cold sweat, ran off his face and mingled with the blood pool, on the in-fill stones, between the train rails.

Almost silence, the hammering outside had stopped. Inside her heart still pounded, her breath gasping air, gulping to draw some more into her lungs.

She fell to her knees, collapsing onto her side. Anto moaned and sobbed,. She thought he was trying to say stop, but only sobs of pain came out from his mouth, bloody also now where he had bitten his tongue and dug his teeth into his lips, red rich, foaming, bubbly blood.

The big man stood up, panting, out of breath. Slowly, with menace, he spoke to Anto. "The next time I will kill you. Find some hole and crawl into it and hope that I don't fall in on top of you some night. OK!"

He turned towards her, took her left hand and placed it on the cold rail. She tried to struggle free but he held her tight forcing her down with his body weight, digging his groin into her back, she could feel her nipples harden against the cold stones.

"You fucked up as well. Now you will have to work for your fixes, now that this shaggers free supply is gone. Just to remind you though!"

She saw him start to raise the hammer. He crashed the hammer down crushing her middle fingers onto the rail.

As the pain hit her befuddled brain she realized, this is real, this is not another trip, she screamed and still screaming fainted.

As O'Neill walked away Traonach materialized out of the shadows beside the disused signal box.

"All clear." He said softly.

"Have you the info on the accountant?"

"Yes."

"Well feckin' give it to me then," O'Neill said with impatience, the adrenaline still coursing through his veins.

"His name is George Bowen. He has an office in Croft Square. He commutes from down the country, Port Siney each day. I'd say that is where he has the priest, in the house, Bowen Court. It's big and rambling, lots of outhouses."

"What does he drive?"

"He doesn't. He takes the train. That's how we tracked him so quickly. He is a creature of habit, follows a timetable you could set your watch to."

"Well, when , where and how?"

"We could go in during the day, when he's away, but we might not find the priest, he probably has him stashed somewhere and besides during daylight we might attract unwanted attention. I'd say go in after he comes home."

He held the car door open for Shane as both stopped to listen to the now faint sobbing.

"I've changed my mind. Get someone to pick them up and stash them. We might still need them." O'Neill ordered.

"Consider it done." Traonach whistled softly into the darkness and when the answering notes came, pointed back towards the tracks and made a pick up and hold gesture.

A lesson learned O'Neill thought. He has his watcher too. Probably watching me.

As if he read his mind Traonach said "He's not watching you. He's protecting you. I owe you a bailout since Derry."

For the first time since he came back to Ireland Shane laughed. "You do. Did you ever get all of the pellets out of your arse?"

"Most of them. You could have yelled keep yer head down, instead of winging me in the arse with the shotgun."

"If I could see yer arse sticking up out of the grass, The Brits firing at us could as well."

"Yea I suppose. anyway that's all over now."

"Yea. All over. Let's get Bowen tomorrow evening. Can you be ready with all the gear we might need? Can we go in as Gardaí? We won't have any trouble getting the priest to come with us if he believes we're the law."

Chapter 24

"It's a country estate," Traonach began, unrolling the ordinance survey map onto the table. "This is the boundary wall at the front: the main gate here he keeps locked - big chain. This here along the wall to the East is a wicker woven gate: smaller chain. We could go in there, it might be a better escape route as it's beside the road."

"Alternatives?"

"Along here there is a boreen around the walled garden with another small gate at the north-east corner. It's well away from everything and we could get in from this farm track . It leads to only one dwelling. About a quarter of a mile before that: it's within one small field of the gate."

"Any others?"

"I don't think we should come in through the woods it's overgrown and clear of that it's a run through the open fields. Anyone could get injured falling over a hillock or stumbling into a rabbit hole and we might have to abandon the job."

O'Neill had his mind made up. "I think in through the garden is the best approach. Once we are inside the wall, here, we're covered. It's only a stroll to the house. What's that like?"

"It's boarded up in places and there seems to only be a few rooms occupied. I watched early this morning as they woke up and the only lights I saw were in the garden houses and in the coach house. We will have to decide how we get into the buildings, when we get down there. I didn't have the time to do the full job and I was afraid if I went to close someone inside might cop-on."

Just like briefings in the North O'Neill thought, precise, complete, accurate and always with options. Traonach had lost none of his skill, and it was well worth sending him down to check the place.

He was a great man for blending in, never looked out of place. Sometimes people swore he was in the farming lark, other times a business man.

His name Corncrake, this one-time chameleon of the hay fields, was well selected.

He had come straight back up to the briefing and was dressed as a surveyor in a high visibility jacket. Even now he was still wearing the hard hat and carrying his files: staying in the role he called it.

The town was growing at a fantastic rate. The population had doubled with the commuters. A surveyor planning for another spate of building now went unnoticed in the place.

Traonach took up the briefing outlining the individual tasks, assigning responsibilities, tying up any loose ends as he spoke.

O'Neill found his attention slipping. Other pictures entered his mind. His mother young, innocent, worrying about her mother in Lourdes, confused, having to be the mother instead of the child, caring, making decisions for the first time in her life.

Mahon, older, more world wise, predatory, comforting and in the end after his needs were filled, cold, dismissive, clerical, uncaring.

It must have been like that, otherwise she would have told him. She must have carried terrible guilt around all her life, every day, every hour. Once again the rage inside started to build, his revenge would be slow, he would make Ahab pay. He heard a distant voice inquire "You all right Boss?"

The small group had turned to face O'Neill, waiting. Traonach sensing his confusion. "Right , we go this evening. Traonach, get back down there, recheck the way in and out. Meet us back at the farm track at eight and lead us in. You two will continue up the lane to the farmhouse and make sure no one comes down near us. You, get a lorry and stick it into the wall at the top of the lane after we go down it. Steal it, crash it, block the lane and run. You will be picked up at this bridge on the way out. We will go in at?" He looked at Traonach. "Eight?"

Traonach nodded. "Eight, on the button. You and you will be outside the gate at eight twenty, dressed in Garda uniforms in the squad car pointed at Dublin. We will come out toss the priest in to you, the boss will get in and the job is Oxo. If there's any mopping up to do I will do it. Now go and get something to eat and get back her in an hour, and boys, no drink! Remember!"

Chapter 25

When Bob reached his office Chief Superintendent Doyle had already beaten him to the fax machine and was reading the report from the Port Siney Gardaí.

"What did the local boys turn up?"

"Very little, are you sure about this guy? He seems to be a pillar of the society," Doyle shook his head and handed over the single page.

The information was scanty and told him little more than he already knew. He noted that Bowen was an accountant with an office in Croft Square. That was not far from Saint Joseph's. Apart from that, the fax added nothing new.

"Is there anyway we can get more Intel without tipping him off? I'd hate to go barging in there to find nothing. We don't want that kind of press."

He's always thinking of how things will look and how they might mitigate against his prospects Bob thought. But he has a point. Cross of Christ! I know this is the guy but I better get me skates on and get some proof. He lifted the phone and rang the Port Siney shop.

"Port Siney. Hello."

"My name is Bob Tyrell. Who's that?"

"Superintendent, it's Harry Roycroft. How are you?"

"Harry is that where you are now? Back home. It must be nice to be back home, after it all. How's the form?"

"Much better than when I tried to mark you in midfield. I'm surprised I don't still have the bruises."

"You were good at dishing it out too, Harry. I'm surprised I still have kidneys that function!"

"What can I do for you Bob?"

"You have a guy down there George E. Bowen, what can you tell me about him?"

"Was it you, looking for the info' I faxed, Bob?"

"It was, but it's not telling me anything. Is there anything else? Anything unusual?

"No, just what was on the sheet. He's a bit odd, keeps to himself, but he's harmless."

Bob went over in his mind what he knew about Harry and even though they had not kept in contact he knew he could trust him with the next question.

"Harry keep this to yourself. Could he possibly be the kidnapper? Of the priest?"

"Christ! Jesus! He wouldn't be top of my list for something like that. Have you anything to go on Bob?"

Quickly Bob filled him in.

"I'm surprised, but he is afraid of dogs I saw it myself and I suppose he could be up to anything in that house and on that estate: if he was quiet. There are a lot of outhouses. We searched them a long time ago when the mother disappeared. Eventually she was found wandering around by the river miles away. She never recovered. She's in some home now: if she is still alive, that is. If Georgie was quiet up to that point, he became almost a recluse after that. He goes to Dublin, to his office on the train, up and back every day. Tell you what Bob, I'll ramble down there and see if I can pick anything up. I can drop into my place first and get a civvies coat and hat and bring the dog for a walk around by the estate and nose around. Georgie won't be back down home for a couple of hours. Would this help?"

"Spot on, Harry. I know I don't need to say it, but keep quiet about this."

"Mums the word, Bob."

Harry moved towards the public office where his single staff member was compiling the seasonal gun license reminder list.

"Can you keep an eye on the phones for a while, I just have to check something out. Do you know where the pair of bins are I may need them?"

The Garda reached down under his counter and handed the battered binocular case to his Sergeant and thought, once he's out of the way I'll warm me arse on his fire for a while. It might warm me up, the draft in this public office is wicked.

Harry always like the river walk. He often came here and let the murmuring, soothing, sounds of the water running over the stones, down the glides, and through the reed beds comfort and strengthen him. The river was his AA companion and the walk his AA meeting.

Now he stood with his back to the bank, partially hidden behind a tall, old, beech tree and scanned the house and out buildings through the binoculars. Christ! It's gone to rack and ruin! It's falling down! You can't see it from the road, but it's knackered.

Slowly, he scanned the boarded up windows, the bricked up back entrance and the off-centre, leaning, chimneys.

He swept the binoculars across, back, up and down the building. From this angle it was a dead, boarded-up, ruin, he wondered how Georgie lived in it at all. Maybe he's not living in the house at all, maybe, he's in one of the outbuildings.

He stood back, checked on the dog, and whistled softly,

the setter returned to his side. He bent down and rubbed vigorously across her head and softly pulled one ear. "Sorry, girl, he apologized as he clicked the leather lead to her collar, "it's softly, softly, from here on."

The wood was overgrown with snagging brambles and waist-high ferns, these obstacles and having to stop constantly to untangle the dog's lead from the undergrowth, slowed his progress. It took him almost twenty minutes to cross through the wood to a point where he could see the outbuildings. He crouched, told the dog to sit and brought the glasses to his eyes, as he sharpened the focus he was disappointed to see that they were also boarded up.

Where are you living Georgie? He checked along the drive toward the estate gates. A gate in the high wall bordering the garden caught his attention. He remembered the search for the mother. The garden? The gardeners' cottages? That's it! To check he needed to go back through the wood, along by the river, and find some way to get up on the high wall.

The garden was the traditional four acre enclosure, the cottages faced eastwards and the garden was protected from the elements by a very high wall.

He checked his watch – it was getting late. By the time he got back through the wood and over to the eastern boundary, he might have little enough daylight for an observation. There was an alternative. He considered the risk of just breaking cover from the wood and walking boldly across behind the house.

It was worth it he decided: Georgie was away, there were no longer servants in the house, no one could call since the main gated were locked, and he would never be seen from the road.

He released the dog from the lead, made a clicking noise to put her on notice that work was at hand, and pointed forward and said. "Go! Girl. Seek!

He waited, while the dog got her bearings and with nose low and tail high she moved out and began her first weaving hunt. He rose and stepped boldly out from the cover of the trees.

He was conscious that he should walk quickly across the meadow and make for the gate where the field met the wall of the garden. Somewhere over there he remembered was a back gate from the garden to the boreen that once went to the gamekeepers cottage at the furthermost edge of the estate.

The house was now abandoned. The Wiggy had lived there alone since Joe and The Mother died but now he was also dead.

Harry remembered how they had broken down the door after Wiggy had been missed in his usual haunts around the town.

They found him dead, cold, alone and ripe on the stone floor of the kitchen an empty blackened pan that they all agreed had once held rashers, sausages, eggs and bread either on it's way to or from the Stanley Range, still grasped in his left hand.

The boreen was so grown over and narrow that two men carried the coffin down to the house and four of them carried it, shoulder high, back to the road.

He started to relax as he approached the gate and the wall, he looked around and whistled to call the dog back.

He made her sit, while he climbed over the gate and turned onto the boreen and back towards the garden. He turned back, slapped his leg and said. "Come." Obediently she came through the lower gate bars and he bent and snapped the lead once more into place and tied it to the side gatepost. "Won't be a minute," he whispered as he moved to check the wall for a vantage point to continue his spying mission.

Chapter 26

Traonach arrived back in Port Siney, parked the car in the town square outside the Weighbridge Inn, and walked back through the narrow Main Street to Bracklone.

Since he knew it was bin collection day he was now wearing a grey Laois County Council jacket that proclaimed in large letters at the back, that he was the Tag Inspector.

A large pair of blue waterproof trousers, baggy and ground hugging at the leg ends: completed the picture of an old, out to pasture, tired, worn out and bored official.

Periodically he halted to examine the empty large black bins for their blue 'I have paid my waste charge ticket' and pushing his glasses high on the bridge of his nose with the middle fingers of his right hand, tried at the same time, to scribble in the black stiff-backed folder he carried.

As he checked the Commuters' bins, which were always left kerbside, until they returned home in the evening: he noticed that commuters paid their charges and tagged their bins. The local were not as law-abiding: helped no doubt by a generous Christmas donation, to the rubbish collectors.

Half way down the village he entered the small farm track and walked slowly toward the distant farm buildings.

A short way down, when he was sure he could not be observed from the road, he sat and removed the jacket and waterproof trousers, and buried them and the folder deep in one of the sodden, overgrown, ditches that always border small badly drained fields.

Underneath, he was dressed in full camouflage

coveralls; a snug fitting bandanna scarf covered his head and he carried a short barrelled, semi automatic weapon, grasped firmly and held tight to his chest. He was already moving quickly, crouched and covered by the hedgerow, towards the gate of the walled garden.

The dog appeared in his line of frontal vision first, just beyond the wall perimeter: then he heard the man whistle.

He threw himself sideways into the ditch at the butt of the hedge. Turning his upper torso, he brought the gun to bear on a depression in the adjoining hedge: that looked to be a hunters' gap.

Shit! If the man crossed the boreen and came over into this field he would have to take action.

He would be to far away to run and attack him. Shit! Feck! Even if it was only the bloody dog that came into the field, and became curious, he would have to react.

Why did I bring the bloody gun, at all? I was only supposed t be nosing around! We're screwed if I fire it, even screwed if yer man see it. Bloody, bloody old habits, that die hard. Shit.

He was motionless, controlling his breathing and tensing his body. Briefly, he saw the upper body of the man appear over the gate into the boreen and heard him call the dog.

Please F-off, don't come over the hedge! If he's a hunter, he might have a shotgun!

He sighted the gun half a man's height above the gap in the hedge, and got ready.

Chapter 27

Outwardly Jim Gaffney had capitulated and settled into the routine imposed upon him in captivity. He rose, attended his solitary breakfast alone in the dining room: always the same toast, marmalade : served in dishes, no labels to identify local or national products and tea, often cold.

He spent the rest of the morning reading the books in his room: the Bible, The Canals of the South of Ireland, The Diocese of Kildare and Leighlin, various publications from the Proceedings of the Huguenot Society, Country and Town in Ireland under the Georges, History of the Queen's County, Coins and Tokens of Ireland, and The Williamite Confiscation of Ireland, along with a series of various privately printed pamphlets and books.

Most of the books had underlined passages or were annotated where some mention, however brief, of various Protestant Families, and their influence on Irish History was recorded.

When his captor realized Jim was reading these books, a game of mental gymnastics begun. On returning to his room after dinner Jim would find a book open at a page that contained a passage designed to annoy or browbeat him, the Act of William and Mary, which required the clergy to swear the following oath, was such a passage.

I do solemnly and sincerely, in the presence of God, profess, testify and declare, that I do believe, that in the sacrament of the Lord's Supper there is not any transubstantiation of the elements of bread and wine into the body and blood of Christ, at or after the Consecration thereof by any person whatsoever.

Since the consecration was such an integral part of his mass – at first this upset him and he threw the book at the wall.

In fairness though, he knew and had to admit, the Dogma of Transubstantiation was not a teaching of the early church. It took the Hierarchy over 1000 years to come up with the idea. The Fourth Council of the Lateran, in 1215, spoke of the bread and wine as "transubstantiation" into the body and blood of Christ.

But in 1625 Galileo asked - if it changes, than why does it taste the same? *Is that the real reason why he was excommunicated?*

Jees, Confession was an open, in the community affair, for the first six hundred years, or so, as well!

Who said it was better to forgive sins against the Community, by hiding them away, whispered between a sinner and a priest, in a box?

Jim began to leave the books in the confession box, on the landing or on the dinner table. He thought this might win some points and tell his captor, to stuff his books, where the 'Sun don't shine'.

In return they kept turning up where he least expected: usually when he was searching around for some means of escape, seeking a weakness in his prison or trying to find some item that might be turned into a weapon.

He decided to continue the mind games and began to scan the book to see if there might be any message in there – he might like to return.

On the day he discovered Elizabeth's letter to the Lord Lieutenant, the Earl of Sussex of May 1559, he sent a retort. *Our two counties of Leix and Offaly do yet remain unstablised and uninhibited, being planted only with men of war wherby they lay waste, without populating, and our charge is likely to grow daily more intolerable.* He wished he had a means of underlining the last part.

When he left the book open at... *This people against whom we fight hath able bodies, good use of arms they carry, boldness enough to attempt, and quickness in apprehending any advantage they see offered them.* The history book did not re-appear.

He felt he had scored a few points and won that particular round. Sometimes he left other books lying around open at suitable passages. Today he had decided to leave the last words to Oliver Cromwell. *Lest the English must needs run away from pure beggary and the Irish possess the country again.*

Jim now knew that eleven girls had been brought to the house, and when they failed to pass Georgie's test of loyalty: to stay and obey and love forever, he had killed them.

It was a simple and deadly approach: he picked hitch-hikers up at the side of the road, when he encountered an opportunity.

Once he got them into the car he used his charm to persuade them to break their journey to visit the estate and Grammy. When he got the girls into the house for tea and cakes he drugged and imprisoned, and eventually killed each one.

Secretly, he buried them in the grounds, in the wood. The surprising thing was that over the years, in the ensuing searches for the missing girls, no report had been received that any witness, had picked up a clue, that would lead the police to his door.

After the outburst, when Jim questioned the sins against the sixth commandment, he had learned to keep his comments and questions brief, and non committal.

Progress was being made. In a few confessions he had learned most of the story and was becoming a little more in control of the session as he was now able, by silence, to elicit information without asking for it.

The major problem he had was that information was now coming so fast that he was struggling to remember it all.

This was not the usual confession approach of each Saturday night or Feast day. He had, long ago, formed a habit of not really listening at all, trigger words would get a response from him, but in general he was not listening and would give a standard penance: one Our Father and three Hail Marys.

These confessions were hard work, a time to be on his toes, and careful, in how he responded. He felt that he was now building up some kind of picture of the abductor.

During a session, to try and cause annoyance and perhaps some kind of slip, he constantly used My Son. Is that all My Son? For penance say a decade of The Rosary My Son. When he was really pissed off. Do The Stations of the Cross My Son.

Almost from the start he suspected that the sinner was not Catholic. The way he approached confessing, his form and rite of words were forced, remembered, not a natural approach of a middle aged person used to confessing, frequently, or even once a year.

The formula he was sure was one gained from listening to other people speak of their experiences. The outburst over the Sixth Commandment convinced him. Some ghost, some driven force, intruded into the box that evening.

The constant use of the title My Son had finally worked. "Don't call me that! My name is George. I am NOT YOUR SON!"

Chapter 28

Georgie was feeling so much better, on-top of the situation, relieved and becoming clean in soul and mind.

Each evening after the confession he felt refreshed, light, and forgiven, sometimes now before bedtime he could stand outside again, admire the sky, the stars and the moon and listen to the night-sounds in the wood, without feeling dirty and upset, or thinking of what was there and how they came to be there.

He had even decided not to burn the house with himself, Grammy and the priest inside. He was he believed starting a new phase of life one where he would be happy – perhaps even live the days he had left happily. A cure might be possible. He would seek out other doctors: specialists maybe.

The woman on the train, Brigitte, the attractive French woman, had waved at him in greeting, they had talked easily and parted with an unspoken promise to meet again.

He had seen her again this morning and waved a greeting. Tomorrow night he would go to the hotel for a drink and maybe bump into her.

Maybe this time he would find happiness. She was older, more mature, would understand him better. He had felt she was lonely also. He went to his room and slept and dreamed of Brigitte.

The dinner was almost over when she reached across the table, thanked him for his company and a lovely meal, and held his hand and asked him to come up to her room and stay the night.

His groin stiffened and hardened as he said yes. His stomach surprisingly filled with lightness as she took his hand and they walked up the staircase.

Champagne and Cognac stood ready on the night stands as they slipped naked between the sheets.

He took the glass and toasted her. She toasted him and leaned forward for a kiss. He turned to return the empty glass to the stand.

He turned back to see her glide towards the bathroom. She turned back and smiled. 'Won't be long,' she laughed, as the overhead lights dimmed down until the room was dark.

The bathroom door opened and softly closed as in the darkness he felt her weight on the bed beside him.

Eagerly he reached out and held her. She urged him to mount her and shifted her position to assist him. He closed his eyes as he felt her body accept and draw him in. He began the slow in and out thrusting with his hips.

No! No! He moaned as his anxious body spilled seed to soon.

He heard her voice, gruff, scolding. Not again Georgie! Not again. You impure boy. You have spilled our seed: wasted OUR seed.

He opened his eyes as the brightness dazzled him and his eyes adjusted and he saw Mumsie lie naked , impaled beneath him, her eyes wild as her red-ruby mouth spit out the words OUR seed.

Like all the other nights: in all the other dreams, he began perspiring, shivering, crying, sobbing and muttering himself back to sleep.

Until the commotion Jim had forgotten that the baby
monitor was still in his room. He woke from the same dream
he was having all his sleep time now: his time being of use
as a confessor and absolver was over; he was dead, but not
unaware; lying in a shallow grave, with the dry taste of earth
in his mouth, and a heavy pressing weight on his eyelids.

Always he tried to open his eyes but couldn't. He tried
to spit the clay out – but couldn't. He tried to stand up –
again the terrible weight of his grave swathes, prevented
him.

But this horror was not his. The sobbing was not his.
The voice calling for Mumsie was not his. Jim listened, the
voice calmed, and began to explain.

"It wasn't me Mumsie, the girl made me. She told me
how to do it, how to take off my clothes and hers and lie her
down and kiss her and IT was hard. IT was hurting me with
the stretching. When she rolled the skin back, IT was not
sore. She took IT and bent IT down, between her legs and
put IT into HERS. I didn't do it Mumsie it was her. I know
she is the help, not like us, but she made me do those things.
No Mumsie I did NOT like it. No Mumsie I WON'T do it
again, ever again. NO!Yes Mumsie I know. Our seed is for
our own kind. Yes Mumsie. Yes. Yes."

The voice was trailing off into sleep again when it
continued. "Yes Mumsie I will think nice things, not scary
things, and they will make me sleep. Yes I will make up a
poem. Yes that will help."

Chapter 29

The warming sun was reaching deep into his prison. The walls radiated back the heat. No advancement had been made in Jim's escape plan: but he still had hope.

The Westminster Chimes called him to his daily duty. Because of the diet, the exhaustion, and the monotony of the ritual, Jim almost missed the statement when his captor made it.

"Bless me Father, for I have sinned. This is my last confession Father. I am going to kill a priest of God, Father, for this sin as with all the sins of my past life, I will be heartily sorry."

Jim had been waiting for this, dreaded it, but was ready. "I can't absolve a sin, if you are not contrite. If you do not have a firm purpose of amendment, not to sin again in that way. I can't give you absolution for murder if you intend to continue murdering! By telling me you intend to murder again, you can't be contrite. All our work, up to now, is ruined. I withdraw the absolution and your soul is as black and rotten as it ever was." Jim raised his voice to emphasise the last phrase, repeating, "As rotten as ever it was."

He wanted George to believe him, because he didn't believe himself. In what he hoped were solemn tones he added."Jesus told us that whatsoever a priest binds on Earth will be bound in Heaven. So that's the end of it!"

Georgie was confused. This was not the way it was supposed to go. He was to be made clean again. This priest was here to make him whole and clean.

This rule was not one he knew, but somewhere down deep inside he knew it must be true. It even made some sense, besides he wanted to stop killing, it was time to stop. He wished Mumsie was here to tell him what to do.

Suddenly he left the confession box: his head was starting to hurt; one of Mumsie's migraines was coming on. He had to think. Mumsie said he was never good at thinking things out: he got that from her, she was the same.

Jim heard Georgie leave the confessional and he sat and waited. Any attack would have to come from in front. He was prepared to fight, even kill, to secure his freedom.

He heard movement. The door restraint was drawn back and he heard footsteps moving away. Cautiously he moved out into the deserted corridor, then ran to his quarters. He closed the door behind him and fell onto the bed.

He pulled his confessional stole: the only reminder of the Good Friday Eve confessions, from around his neck, and threw it on the floor.

He watched it fall. The symbol of his authority to the magic act of forgiveness, of cleansing penitent solace.

Some solace you are for me. You are no better than a football scarf now.

The European Championship, and the World Cup – Jack's Army, entered his mind, scenes of flags on poles and bunting and scarves and flags hanging from windows.

He jumped up from the bed so quickly that his head spun and he fell back to sit on the bed. He rose again. "You fool! It was there all the time, a signal. It could show a priest is in here. Gobshite!"

He scooped up the stole and entered the small alcove toilet. He elbowed a small pane of glass outwards into the bars and towards the wooden shutter boards.

To his surprise the pane fell forward still in one piece, resting on the frame. Gently he eased it upwards from the single remaining bottom putty strip and placed it on the floor. He closed his eyes and drove his right hand, fingers crunched and braced, violently against the wooden board shutter.

He jumped back eyes tear filling, gasping in anguish. Like a hand strapped pupil of his schooldays he tried to warm the torment away: squeezing his knuckles beneath his upper arm, clasped into his armpit.

Clumsily, using his left hand he managed to squeeze the stole through the small sideboard crack: purchased by his pain. He waited for the hurt to ease, and placed the glass pane back into place. This time it was secured by its sole-plate of putty and a header of the material.

It may be foolish, I may be enduring this throbbing in vain, but it's all I have, it's all I can do. Please God. Please, show my flag of freedom to someone and give them the curiosity to investigate it.

Chapter 30

Traonach was surprised when the man came into view again, not coming across the hunters' gap but climbing up the garden wall.

He could clearly see him as he found and placed his fingers in cracks and chips in the mortar that held the stones together and pulled his body upward.

When he had almost reached the top he became cautious and only moved his head upwards so that he could see over the top. Satisfied he braced himself by throwing his upper arm on top of the wall, and balanced himself with that forearm, and the elbow of the other arm which now pressed a pair of binoculars to his eyes.

While Harry Roycroft checked out the old vegetable garden of Bowen Court, Traonach slowly retreated along the ditch until he found what he was looking for. Quickly he crouched up, and leaped over and behind the old railway sleeper cow bridge, linking the two fields. He crawled into the small damp overgrown space beneath the bridge until he was able once again to view the man without being seen himself.

Just at that point – as if warned by that hidden instinct we all have, that seems to warn us we are being watched: Harry turned his head and checked out the fields behind him. Slowly deliberately he quartered the space, checking but not finding the source of his unease.

Still suspicious, not satisfied with that his eyes were failing to find, he suddenly dropped from the wall and from view.

Traonach pushed himself into the centre of his cave

beneath the bridge. He suspected now that this man, was the law and if given the chance, would be an adversary to fear.

He checked his watch and decided to give it the best part of an hour before venturing out. He decided to take extra care. The law is on to this fello' as well, but they are still only checking things out. They are not sure!

Sixty five minutes later he was in the garden with the old wooden door back in place; now, instead of hanging on it's hinges it was propped in place by the inside plank of the door-jam.

This delay, he had encountered, was not serious and he knew that he had a few minutes over an hour to locate the priest and plan the best approach for the attack that would free him: into their custody.

Chapter 31

Bob Tyrell was ready to brief the teams. Harry Roycroft had reported back.

"I almost missed it Bob. Jeepers! I almost missed it. I thought at first it was a football flag, an Irish Soccer flag left hanging there. But thinking about it, I asked myself why Georgie would hang a flag where no one would see it. I thought – it's new, not faded, like the others you see all washed out after weeks in the weather. I focused in on it and knew it wasn't a flag. It wasn't a flag shape. It looked to be tailored, finished with more care, but I couldn't place what it was. It moidered me all the way back here. At school I remembered, being marched out by The Brothers for monthly confession, then when I was an altar boy I watched the priest dressing for Mass. I remembered my numbed fingers in religion class for not being able to name the vestments. It came to me again: The Amice, The Alb, The Cincure, The Girdle and The Stole; it's a stole, Bob. The priest was wearing it in confession when he was taken. Now he's hanging it out of Georgie's gardeners' cottages to signal where he is being kept."

A quick look at Learscailspeir.Com, the Irish Language mapping service, on the Net provided aerial photographs that confirmed the location of small buildings, in the walled garden at Bowen Court.

The house, wood the outlying pathways and the boreens together with the perimeter wall were clearly visible. It was even possible on zoom-in and make out the front gateway.

Bob decided he would have a quick search to see if he could find out any more about Bowen Court. He brought up Google and typed his query, it's funny he thought that it should now be a word to look at things: in my day we often asked to have a Goggle at a paper or a picture.

Within a few minutes Bob had pictures of the house, as it had been two years ago when it was advertised for sale. He had also had discovered the failed planning permission for houses and apartments and a blurb on the history of the house from the local district tourism site.

He considered his next move: there was no real proof, except what Harry thought was a priest's stole in a window. It could just as well be a rag with green mildew on it, but they had damn all to go on so far and doing something stupid was better than doing nothing at all.

Cross of Christ it would be better to go in and find nothing than to have this thing drag on forever as a missing person case: just like the rest. It was a stole that Harry saw. If I can convince myself of that; I can convince The Chief to let us go in. It WAS was a stole! So it was!

Big blow ups of the maps and the pictures were on the white board in the briefing room, scattered ashtrays cups and mugs, had been pushed to a small corner table and the team once again went over the notes of the last two hours.

"Right lads, we will go in at four in the morning. You all know what to do, this is the kind of thing you are trained for." Bob looked around the room at the team.

"The local Gardaí are sure, it's a one man job: Bowen on his own. They say he's solitary. But still watch out. You could hide an army in these bushes here at the front of the house. We go in by the wicker gate. Group Alpha will move around the stables here, get in under the walkway from this building to the main house, and cut off anyone bolting out towards the wood. Bravo, Ryan's group, will move up to the main door and try to kick it in. Hopefully you will be nothing more than the diversion. Fanahan and Mc Gill are with me in Charlie."

He looked over to where Fanahan was talking to someone on a phone.

"Detective, am I keeping you from some more urgent business?" The phone was slammed down. "Jees someone has a sore ear now!" *Fanahan will get a thick ear if he continues sulking!*

"We get into the garden, through the arch and into the house across the walkway, from these outhouses. Harry Roycroft will be with us. He says we can easily pull the boards off the windows on the lower level. If we can't get in, we will double back and come in the front door: after you guys have knocked it into the hall. I know it's a shitty plan compared to others we have used, but we can't risk any more delay, and we have to go in now. A delay while we foolproof the plan could be disastrous. Just be as careful as you can, and for all our sake, don't fire at any target, unless it's armed and, listen to me now: don't hit the priest. One last thing. Roycroft got one of his feelings, that he was being watched as he spied the place out. He didn't see anyone. It could have been the local Peeping Tom at the back of these other houses, but be aware, unlikely as it is, that someone else may be on to Georgie. For all we know Bishop Mahon may be up to his old tricks, trying to organise a hand-over. It wouldn't surprise me if he had a private Seamus Shoval on the job."

Inwardly his mind was once again trying to get ahead of the game. *If Mahon is negotiating because the kidnapper contacted him that's one thing, but if he has someone down there snooping around, from where, or who from, did he get his bloody information.*

"Cross of Christ!", he said out loud as the team looked quizzically at him, "be back here, ready to go, fed and watered, in two hours. Sergeant, get Harry Roycroft on the phone for me, please"

Chapter 32

Jim attended for confession as usual, 'On the morrow' as instructed by the disembodied baby-monitor voice, hoping that Georgie would not notice that his stole, part of his uniform in all the confessional sessions was missing. In the dim light of the cubicles it was unlikely. He knew that at least one of his fingers was broken and he had to endure the constant pain, without supporting the break.

He believed the confession would once again be an attempt to secure absolution for the next crime: his murder. He had his mind ready, fuelled by the pain. He was ready to argue hard.

The voice was different, not as assured as it had been, the tone was new uncertain and afraid.

"Pastor" it began, " Mumsie said I had to tell you about the farm girls and what they made me do. How they robbed our seed."

The dream Jim thought it's what he said in the dream.

"Mumsie wants me to be forgiven for what I did. I promise I won't do it again. Am I forgiven Pastor?"

"For this transgression only. Yes you are forgiven."

"Thank you Pastor."

His abductor left the box. Jim was alone with new thoughts rushing through his head. What the Feck, just happened was the one uppermost and unanswered.

He sat and tried to fit the pieces into the new jigsaw. He had his old pieces in place: he was chosen and brought here to attend the confession of a murdered because that killer believe a priest could make him clean.

He had those bits, had them for a while: abductor, priest, confessor, sinner, murdered, but now a new piece, child.

What The Feck! The chimes called him to the meal. *Shit! All I really need now is for The Duchess to sing Old Man River.* He tugged on his leg restraint and walked towards the dining room.

The seating ritual was ignored. The Duchess did not appear to be herself: her regal stride was faltering, her manner not as haughty as usual. She sat quickly, not waiting for him to rise and greedily drank the wine that was usually sipped and savoured as a digestive aid.

Is she in need of a drink to keep her going? I wonder was she at the sherry: is that it? For the first time her table manners were less that impeccable. She cropped audibly at her salad, her lips retaining the juices of the tomatoes and vinaigrette, pieces of food escaping from her mouth to spot the tablecloth and her usually impeccable dress front.

Her napkin, unused, he was sure – even unnoticed, still lay within its restraint on the table.

She hardly reacted when the door behind Jim was thrown open and the armed men entered the room. A hand pulled him to his feet and tried to drag him towards the door. His restraint fouled against the chair and the man's feet. He looked down briefly, moved his body to the front, loosened the tangle and pushed Jim towards the door.

The Duchess, by now has slumped face down, onto the table. One of the men moved towards her and raised his gun. The man holding Jim growled "No! Leave her. Out!"

Jim watched the scene in slow motion as he was thrown out into the corridor, falling onto his hands and knees.

He tried to rise and he smelled the cordite, and felt the heat of the handgun shot, as the leg restraint shattered. The force and velocity knocked his left leg sideways, numbness more than pain made him fall over again.

The sound of the shot was soft, muzzled by the silencer, the whine of the ricochet was loud. The smoke-puff of dislodged plaster where it hit the ceiling accompanied the loud footsteps fast and pacey, on the bare floorboards. He was lifted and dragged out into the evening air.

Grammy had been enjoying these interludes with the Parson,. A nice polite, quiet, mannerly young man, if a bit shabby in his dress, obviously unmarried. From the look of him badly in need of an increase in his stipend. She would talk with Major Bowen and see if he could ask the other landowners to consider upping the emolument.

She knew she was getting old, because now she recalled little of her day except dressing and attending this dinner. Today, unusually she recalled that Frances had spoken to her about the boy. She was anxious because she thought he was mixing again.

It was no matter. If he only moved among them, and learned of their life: their existence would be a more correct word, that was fine, but if he was mixing, it would have to stop.

They had lost the pure seed once, in the boy, and now if he went unchecked he might de-sanguine the line.

Certainly before the boy there had been a few indiscretions, but that was long ago, and the purity of the line was not at that time entrusted to her.

It would have to stop. The food was indifferent, bland: she would have to reprimand the kitchen staff. The wine was passable: she was quaffing frequently however. It would not do, in the presence of the Parson.

When the brigands, entered the room she tried to rise and protest, but the vapours overcame her. When she recovered they had gone and taken the Parson with them. Fearing their return, she knew she must hide: her childhood refuge! Where she was safe so long ago! If she could find it now?

It was only when she was hidden in the dark comfort of the hidden nook behind the wall in the confession box that her pounding heart slowed, her breathing became longer and filled her lungs once again with oxygen and the vapours subsided.

She dozed uncomfortably and became hot. She considered leaving her haven.

When she heard the brigands return, she trembled and like so long ago, when she hid the boy here; away from the fury of Bowen, just like the boy used to do – she sobbed quietly.

Chapter 33

Bob and his team waited just outside the town for the morning light to drive the shadows of night away. Then in the misty morning twilight drove slowly into the long street and past the path side boundary wall. Bob saw the empty archway at the same time that Fanahan swore.

"Shit Boss. The gate is down!"

When Fanahan saw the gate lying against the privet hedge inside the archway in the wall: his adrenaline soared. He checked the gun and moved slowly forward. He motioned with a low backward motion of his left hand: indicating where the gate lay. It had been moved there, he reasoned after the hinges were severed, carefully moved, not thrown.

Whoever, did that took their time in a stealthy approach. It occurred to him that perhaps the gate was not the way in: maybe it had been the way out. He moved forward while Bob came behind.

If anything moves I'll blast away and ask questions later. Crouched-over, bent-legged, they sprinted, singly across the drive, covering and protecting each other.

Their progress was silent, the gravel that would once have betrayed their approach had long ago surrendered to the weeds, and the scutch-grass.

The front door was half open, the hallway dark, the interior quiet.

Fanahan stood, inhaled deeply and briefly held the air in. He listened, turning his head, slowly he exhaled, took another deep breath and entered the house.

Bob followed.

Thirty minutes later they walked back out the front door, across the drive and the lawn, through the wicker arch and reported back.

"The shaggin' place is like a morgue, they fecked off!"

"We can't even determine if the priest was held there."

We have a slim chance left, Bob decided, as he spoke. "As soon as it's brighter, get the forensic team down. Go over it in detail, and get some fingerprints or anything to show us that this is the right place. Cross of Christ!"

When Grammy was sure at last, after so long a time, that the second band of brigands had vacated the house, only when she believed the coast was clear: did she leave her hiding place. She went looking for the boy, but as usual whenever she needed him he was missing again.

The brigands had upset things in her room, but she was able to find fresh togs, and recover some of her composure. A Lady will conduct herself as a lady in all circumstances, especially those trying ones she encounters.

She spent some time, waiting for the boy to return. It was at times like this, that he usually returned and tucked her into sleep for the night, but today, despite her tiredness, she could not find her Sandman.

So she sang her soft songs, and waited, and sang again, old songs of the woods and the trees and the wind, and still she waited for the boy to return.

What ever Grammy did now, she did as if in a dream, like a part of her knew a different way of doing things.

She felt uncomfortable at her toilet, at times her clothes hindered her steps, and when seated she was a constant fidget.

Most surprising of all she knew the world outside her

abode although she could never remember visiting that place before.

There was a town, there were people: that perhaps she knew but could not remember knowing. Maybe they knew her and the boy and could help her find him. The strange thing however was that she knew where to find the boy and how to get there.

She dressed appropriately for the train journey to the city, and carefully carrying the boys pocket book, the one he left behind with the money, his business cards and the rail ticket for the journey: for the first time ever she set out on a new adventure, alone without a retinue.

Needs must she thought as she left and walked through the flower gardens and she saw them in full bloom. She enjoyed their perfumed scent at the peak of their season.

She moved beneath the leafy parasol of tree branches and her eyes narrowed, squinting in the sudden brightness, when she moved out onto the avenue towards the train station.

She found a quiet carriage, declining an invitation from a mature well dressed, well spoken, man in a uniform, to enter his carriage. Ignoring his, "This way Madam."

She declined gracefully. Old military men she knew, back from wars, were interesting in conversation, but wayward in their morals and to be avoided where possible. The early morning train was almost empty: the views of the passing scenery was green and lush. The small fields and roads were clothed in their gossamer web of colour textured leaves.

The small stations she passed were brightly painted clean and tidy, the small road-bridge-side gardens were filling with colour.

The air seemed to grow clearer, carrying her eye back to the Slieve Bloom Mountains, as it became a hazy distance pointer of where her journey had begun.

At the terminus she engaged a hackney man, wordlessly indicating her destination, by showing the business card.

In minutes he had delivered her to a small street-side family style residence. She protested that this could not be a place of commerce, but he just shrugged and departed.

She moved up the steps and engaged the bell. A voice asked her business. Startled, but composed she asked for the boy, but in front of strangers she asked for him by name. "Mister Bowen, I'm here to meet Mister Bowen."

"He's not here today. He hasn't come in yet. Come back later."

Confused by perusing a conversation with someone she could not see, outside a door, without a grill or any other visible speaking device, she felt like a common washerwoman at a trades entrance. Nevertheless, she continued. "I must see him, it's a matter of some urgency."

"He's not here yet. Come back after lunch. He might be in then." She heard the girl laugh. "Or he might not be."

Grammy moved back onto the path and stood to examine her surroundings. She would find a tearoom and wait.

Chapter 34

This briefing, back in Dublin, before The Chief was never going to be easy, but Bob managed to get through it. He knew he was expected to buck everyone up and keep some momentum in what was now a damp-squib operation.

In front of the men his superior was quiet, asking positive questions and providing some positive outlook in his own answers.

In contrast the dressing-down he had given Tyrell in the solitude of his own office, had been ferocious and at times out of control. It was obvious that the higher echelons of rank had delivered a similar rebuke to Chief Superintendent Doyle earlier.

"We still have our man to catch, it's not over yet, just because somehow he got on to us and moved the priest and made it harder, now means we have to try all the harder. Shay, Shay! Are you listening?"

Fanahan in fact wasn't listening to Tyrell. What was the point in talking about it all. The bloody house was falling down: a dive, ready for the salvage men. Only a few rooms had been used and the priest was gone from them. He had been there shackled to some kind of low set dado-rail near the floor. It also kept him tethered in some kind of a sleeping area. Only one other bedroom had been used and it was a right mess, they didn't even know if a man or a woman had lived there.

The clothes were suits, trousers, pullovers and long gowns, cologne, after shave, powder, old face power stuff and wigs.

In the only other reasonable room it was obvious that

the priest and the kidnapper had some kind of a meal, even wine, before they cleared off.

If you were to ask Fanahan for an opinion he would have said that by now they were probably buddy boys, maybe even be giving one another hand-jobs, to relieve the boredom of being cooped up in a house down there in the bogs.

That would explain the gowns and the powder puffs, despite his terrible bad humour at the moment, he almost laughed out loud, Puffs!

He knew the skull proders had some kind of name on the affinity that could grow between victim and abductor, ever since it happened to Patty what's her name, who even robbed a bank with her kidnappers,. She got away with it because of the family money. Didn't President Carter commute the prison sentence!

Was it Getty or Hearst? He knew it was some kind of real money that solved the problem, like always there's a lot that money can buy.

Was it Kavanagh? 'Money isn't everything, but a few pounds in the pocket is great for the nerves.' If the tosser had a real job, that kept him out of the pub, he might have held on to some of it. Drink is for after work, to relax and bullshit with a few pals.

He had an uneasy feeling about that house that he couldn't tie down. It was as if he had been there: maybe it was the same house he saw in his childhood nightmares.

He would find himself in the big house, at the top of the long tree lined avenue in the country fields, near the river, with the stuffed animals and birds all over the place.

When he moved through the rooms glassy unblinking

eyes met and followed him. Large outstretched wings blocked his way. Red dog foxes bared their teeth and badgers lurked in corners, spines arched, pelts bristling.

Maybe it was the house, but if it was the stuffed horrors were long gone too. He shivered, as someone shouted at him, and gave his usual save all answer. "Yes Boss."

He was sure that Tyrell, in spite of the stress and tension he was under at present – the bastard, smiled as he handed out the assignment. He pulled a page from his notebook and handed it over.

"Shay. I want you to go down, to this address, and introduce yourself to the nice lady and her dog. When they go out along High Street, I want you to go with them and if the dog gets interested in a man, growls at a man, I want you to bring the man back here."

The shagger smiled again. Feck it! How would he explain this if his new pals on the drug squad got wind of it.

Was your job assignment as a dogsbody? Yea! I was a seeing eye – for a shaggin' seeing eye dog. Bollix!

Tyrell had reconciled himself to the fact that the raid on Bowen Court had come to late and he never believed in crying over spilled milk.

The question that now occupied him was how had it come to late, they acted quickly on the intelligence, but somehow they had been beaten to the punch.

The priest had been there, kept captive there for some time. Bowen had moved Father Gaffney and it was back to square one, looking for another needle in a haystack. Unless Fanahan came across something on the street with Anne and Sheba, this was going to go cold again.

Cross of Christ it was cold again. It was a very long shot. He shouldn't even have Fanahan out on the street it was nonsense to be relying on a dog to growl at someone. It was a real waste to the taxpayers' money, but it was follow this line for a while or shut up shop. But he believed that Bowen was gone – maybe forever.

At the start of all this he had hopes that they might be on track to solve some of 'The Missing' cases. Those people who had disappeared over the years. Now it seemed as if this was a different Modus altogether. They didn't know much about what happened in the other cases, but it was unlikely, that any of them had been kept captive like the priest, chained up somewhere.

He felt this was a different case different emotions at play. If any of the others had been kept captive over time, someone, somewhere would have stumbled onto something.

He felt 'The Missing' were all taken in passion, passion he knew could never be the correct word, but a crime of passion was a way it was normally described.

He thought there should be another word. But what

word could you use to describe some lunatic taking a person raping them, or abusing them, and killing them and being able to dispose of a body where it was never found.

It wasn't passion it was something else. A crime of evil gratification? You could never use that it was to harsh! Inside his head the voice again, the one he had carried with him all his years in the job.

To all of you I'm sorry, I've let you down again. I will keep trying as long as I have breath in my body. Please God, someday soon.

After the team left he slapped the file down on his desk. With his foot he pushed the white-board around towards the wall where he could not read its tale of woe. He pushed his chair back from the desk and placed his legs on the surface; he bent his elbows and placed his palms behind his head and stared blankly out the window, into the blue sky.

Chapter 35

Jim was relieved when he saw the Garda Car and was happy to allow himself be pushed inside. Up to then he has no idea who had liberated him, or if indeed this was liberation. The whole thing had been speed and confusion. He had been considering trying to make a run for it if the chance to flee presented itself. He was confused by the camouflage uniforms of the men and the balaclavas and the guns. He knew very little about guns. These looked different to those he saw on the television when the Arms Trial was mentioned and that footage of the men standing before the Freedom Wall.

These guns looked, sleeker, tidier, more lethal, if that was possible. After all, a bullet from an antique musket could kill you just as dead.

He was happier now. Two uniformed Gardaí and a soldier were taking him away – free from his prison.

He turned to the man beside him and started to say thanks. The man smiled a little and said, "No bother. All in a days work. Just glad to have found you and got you out unharmed. How many of them were there?"

"Just the one and The Duchess."

"The Duchess?"

"The old lady" he explained. "I took to thinking of her as The Duchess ."

" I see and who was the other one?"

"The man, The Sinner. I called him The Sinner. He took me so that he could confess."

"To what?" The man asked softly.

In the days and nights of his captivity because of the confessions Jim had known that if he was released, or

134

rescued, or just got away under his own steam, that this question would be asked.

He did not know how to answer it. The information he got in the confessional was privileged. He was not allowed reveal it.

On the other hand if he never told what he learned, the girls would remain missing. Their relatives, their loved ones, would remain in the dark. It was a dilemma he thought about and hoped it would be a decision, he would welcome having to make in time, because at that time he would be free.

"Things," he replied. "Things I'm not sure I can tell you. It was a confession."

"Well, you better make a quick decision, before the debriefing."

For the remainder of the journey they drove in silence. Left to his own thoughts, beside the priest, in the back of the replica Squad Car, Sonny didn't care what the priest had heard in confession from Bowen.

It was probably some kind of theft, money laundering, or just plain embezzlement, an accountancy scam, about money anyhow. Having the priest, was the important thing not finding out what was in his head.

In Cavan, he had come back down the mountain, his heart as cold as the Druid's Stone that held the secret buried away from him for the long years. He hurried towards the house, angry, waving the papers, to confront his mother. Looking for answers. Looking for justice. Instead when he came in, he was quiet and spoke about Daideo. Later in the twilight, he talked about when he was a boy at night in the light of the oil lamp, when they sat by the window. She told him tales of the mountain and her people before them, feeling in that time now, he asked gently. "Tell me about my father, tell me about Francis Syslvester Mahon."

When she told him he understood and because she had given him life, and reared him, what ever she had kept hidden away at the time, she thought it was for his protection.

He knew now that she was the real victim and had paid a high price, consigned to her lonely life, with her lonely secret, under the gaze of disapproving neighbours and the extended family.

He remembered. Mammy, Daideo and Sonny in the silent days and months. Only funerals brought them out: obligation bound to join the mourners.

When the countryside neighbours had gawked enough and the cousins knew they had attended they cleared off and left them to the gossip.

He hugged her tightly when the time came to leave and turned quickly and left.

He didn't want her to see the resolve in his eyes.

Chapter 36

Now Sonny had the priest, he had his bait, all he needed was to set the trap. An email, he decided, would kick the whole thing off. He would have liked to lure Mahon back to Amsterdam, make him pay the price, get rid of him there. Getting the priest out of the country was a risk he didn't need to take. Besides Holy Catholic Ireland would be a better place for a nice crucifixion.

Who knows? Maybe Mahon could rise again after three days. No you won't rise you bollix! Not when I'm finished with you.

Bishop Mahon was very careful about his personal email address. He never gave it out to anyone except those inside his inner circle of trusted friends.

He never used it on the Internet to buy goods or book hotel accommodation. He did that kind of trade by old fashion means through his secretary. If the message he received had not contained the good news that O'Neill had not only located the priest but had secured his release and was now ready to for the hand-over – he would have been even more furious.

As it was he was determined to find out who spilled. It would never have entered his mind, being computer illiterate, that the Web was a series of vast connections. Once he logged in each evening to check his messages, his Internet service provider, or more accurately the help desk staff at his service provider, would have to know certain details in order to fix any problem he encountered: in his garbled mails, or sudden drop in communication speed.

Recently Mahon had been having lots of annoying

problems and had been calling on their expertise frequently. Help desks, particularly those that offer a twenty-four-seven service can be lonely boring places after midnight and a bit of mental diversion now and then helped.

If the stuff was good, and free – paid for by favours, the boring hours were tolerable, and the weekend fuelled.

The message was simple. 'Have secured release of goods held for clearance. Consignment is in good order will advise collection details later'.

The sender was a nondescript company he had never heard of before and was sure once this was over, never would again.

He replied as nondescript as his pounding heart would allow. 'Thanks for Info awaiting further details'.

He hoped it was all true, that O'Neill had Gaffney safe and ready for the hand-over. He would ensure that the event would be of maximum benefit and publicity: for himself.

He smiled. Back in the big time again – Cardinal Mahon!

Chapter 37

Harry Roycroft was pissed-off. The raid had been a failure and he blamed himself. He should have acted on his gut feeling that he was being watched when he checked out the estate. He should have gone looking, flushed out who ever it was, and even if they did not break cover, he might have scared them off for a while. Then perhaps their operation would have ended differently.

He needed a drink. More that ever before he needed a drink. That would clear his head, he would be able to think, to work this out, to help. He was the local man on the job, he should be able to find something, some clue. He hadn't had a drink for a long time. He knew what the drink did to him, made him angry, argumentative, quarrelsome. Just now he didn't care.

Outside the Forge Inn, the American Tours Courier was describing the location to her circle of multi-green-shaded lemming tourists.

"Foxcroft and Main!" She bawled pointing at the street signs. "We'll meet back here after the free half-hour, thirty minutes, OK! Ya got that?"

She moved both hands in a wide sheep-shooing, go-away, get lost gesture hoping to disperse the flock – so that she could nip into the pub for a throat-soothing, thirst quenching, drink.

Not succeeding, nevertheless she left and entered by the side entrance on Foxcroft Street. They still stood, shuffling, and checking their umbrellas, waterproofs, handbags and cameras unsure of how to use their period of free-range tourism.

Harry ordered a Guinness, and sat and waited at the bar, while it was poured and left for its primary settle. He looked around remembering this pub had been a hardware shop.

There, near that alcove where the counter ended, was the spot where he waited, after being sent down from the upper Kelly Hardware, to get a long stand and some sky hooks. After about fifteen minutes old E.J. chewing his dentures, laughed and asked him if he had been standing long enough. He told him to go back and tell Ronnie that all the sky hooks were in the sky cup-hooking the clouds.

He came out feeling foolish and even now could remember the clear blue cloudless sky, that covered and sheltered him back to his summer job, that year before he left for the Training College in Templemore.

The Guinness arrived, still swirling, brown turning to black, cream head forming and reaching the prescribed depth. He knew it would taste bitter, sour, unusual. He also knew that when he had finished the second pint his taste would be back as savage as ever for alcohol.

The barman asked again, "Will that be all?"

"Yes. Thanks." Harry replied as he offered a note, took the Pint, and turned away.

"The change?"

"The Poor-box." Harry suggested.

The Americans were starting to drift into the bar and were trying to order Sodas. Harry noticed a small ferret faced, sad looking little gentleman, who was standing beside a large rotund woman. She was giving him instructions for her drink, "A soda and some potato chips and some god-damn pretzels. If you can get some in this godforsaken place."

140

Harry moved and stood before the pair. The man looked at him, relief on his face that someone had interrupted the continuous flow. The woman still aggressive asked "Can I help ya buddy?"

Ignoring her Harry handed the pint to the man and said, "Get this into ya. It could help."

Hughie took the offering as his companion tried to take it back from him. "Pudda down Sweetie. Ya don' know where it's bin."

After two weeks of one and two day whistle stop visits on the European Huguenot Trail: Sweetie was not concerned with where it's bin, as he had decided, he knew where it was goin'.

He took a long slow, tasting draught, of the cool Guinness, smacked his lips and for the first time in his married life answered his wife back.

"Shaddap Doris," he said sharply, "Go get yer own god-damn Pretzels."

I should have come here and done this first, Harry thought, as he walked beside the river, the setter hunting along the river side before him: but the poor tourist might still be hen-pecked. I wonder will he keep it up. I'd say he will: that was a fierce look in his eye as he chastised her.

They walked along the river, towards the ruined boathouse on the riverbank, behind the estate. Two swans moved warily downstream, circling every now and then to see if they were being followed.

He remembered that in the wood there was a glade. When he was young and had finished running with his pals cry-echoing through the wood, they would go there and look at Sean de Piquer.

He wasn't sure what the Huguenots meant when they called him that name. It could mean Sean who was pierced, because of the hole in his neck, or just Sean who was put to sleep.

It was a statue of a knight in armour-plate: it was broken into three pieces, the head, the body, the legs with a dog lying at his feet. There were legends about him that he put the shoes on his horse backwards to confuse his enemies and that he was killed by his servant, who pushed an arrow into his neck above his armour, as he watched the ducks flying into the lake.

When he returned back home as Station Sergeant – he was able to call in some favours: after the trauma of the split-up and the binge drinking. When he was still trying to pull his life back into some kind of order and he was lonely – he joined the local Historical Society. It was really a statue of the Constable of Carlow Castle, Robert Hartpoole who died in 1594. It was brought here by a relative of his, a Miss or Mrs. Bowen, when she owned the house. Some say it was brought up the river on a barge. They built a mound, on the hill above the glen and placed the parts to rest on a large black slab.

He stood now on Sean's mound above the glen. Despite the neglect he could still make out how the estate had been organized. He could still see the lake, hidden over the overgrown privet hedge, that also covered the path: the walkway to and from the house. On the left was the farm manager's house, he kept good fighting cocks. He recalled one chase after a cockfight, when he had caught Joe, and realized who it was ,he let him go: off home ya little Scallywag.

That Beech tree up there at the very top of the glade is the one we carved our initials on.

He climbed up the steep well-mulched, forest debris covered hill and started to examine the tree. Yea MMCC, Mick McCann. JH, Hargrove. MR, The Rabbit. McGowan, Dunne, Shortall. Roycroft, Shea, DD, The Dudee, Mac, JC, amazing all still here. Jesus!

Another tree at the top of the glen, an Oak, took his attention. The kids today are still carving initials he thought as he moved closer. These guys were more up market than we were, clearer carving. Our old penknives, legacies of the priest of pipe and plug were always worn-out blunt and wouldn't take an edge.

Who were these? They are not as worn as ours. They're newer. It must have been the next generation of vandals.

Harry read each set out loud. " PS, SD, JS, MD, MW, IM, NOBD, MCS, DB, JG, SF.

He sat down at the butt of the tree looking down at the bracken and wild ferns, overgrowing on a forest floor that he remembered covered in a mulch of small twigs and Pine cones.

At the end of Autumn it lay under the brown and yellow and green leaves. At times cradling the Hawthorn Haws that blew in from the trees on the river bank and the Chestnuts, The Conkers, that they collected and threaded on strings to fight the Conker Wars.

He was relaxed, his AA companions – the river and now the wood had once again soothed him. He was feeling serene even though he was sitting less that a quarter of a mile away from the house, the remorse at what he had thought was his cock-up had ebbed.

Being in the wood where he had played as a child somehow gave his thoughts a childish curiosity.

In all the time he had walked near here, he never once wondered about the statue and where it might have gone. He knew there were rumours that it had been taken away, or that Georgie had thrown it in the river or the lake.

Now sitting here, he became curious once again. I wonder: is the statue of Sean de Piquer still down in the bottom of the glen, among the willows, hidden beneath the generations of leaves and fallen branches?

He whistled for the dog and began to move downward, feet forward, knees bent, trunk lying backward.

Occasionally he fell: but balancing his body, with one hand pushing against the ground, he slithered down until he gained his balance.

When he could stand upright and balanced again, he began to part the pliable wicker canes, eyes downward seeking for the colour change, small mound, or ivy and creeper covered stone that would be one of the three statue parts.

He was still moving forward eyes downcast when he came to the patch of cleared ground, and the hole, freshly opened, with the earth piled grave like beside it. He looked up, puzzled.

Walking forward he noticed the ground was uneven. He reached the hole and stood looking around.

He remembered once, looking at a picture of an old hag with a big chin and a feather in her cap, that suddenly became the profile of an attractive young girl.

Now, he had the same experience. One moment he was looking at a circle of scrub-grass, ferns and brambles, but sweeping his gaze across the clearance, he was looking at eleven depressions, and an open grave.

They lay like the plane of a sundial around a central stone mound. His mind absorbed and processed the information: the stone mound was Sean's statue. The parts were collected and piled together and the clock hands were all graves.

He looked back up at the oak tree and counted the sets of initials. Eleven! Eleven graves? Eleven people - a tombstone for their marker. And an open grave, ready for a new victim. The Priest!

Unaware of the brambles catching at his clothes – holding him as if the wood was making one last effort to preserve its secrets. He stumbled, hurried, ran out from the wood and back towards the Garda Station.

Chapter 38

Bob stood in front of the oak, his back was to the graveyard. The shallow graves lay open and empty. their secret revealed, their occupants now lying on makeshift tables in the county morgue.

He fingered the tree, each set of initials now ticked off on the printout, some of the initials could be for more than one name, he had three SD's, Davis, Douglas or Donovan? Two JG's Grogan, Grennan or Goodwin?

He hoped the forensics would solve that little riddle. At least he knew that eleven of The Missing had been recovered. Eleven bodies that he hoped would soon be identified and handed over to grieving families, for the final closure of knowing – just knowing.

It was imperative now that they find Georgie quickly. He hoped the empty grave meant that he had not killed the priest.

The teams out beating the land, and the boats on the river, so far had not discovered his body. The house was being searched also, it was likely to fall down on their heads if they tore it apart roughly.

The small room behind the confession box was a surprise. They would never have found it, if the panel in the wood had been closed.

He wondered if Georgie had been hiding there when they searched the house the first morning.

The bedroom had been examined. It was presenting them with another mystery. They could not determine if it was essentially a man's bedroom, or a woman's boudoir. It seemed to be both as if a man had shared it with a woman.

No one had mentioned that Georgie had a companion. He had phoned the office staff and asked, but they just laughed. "No Way!" They even giggled in a way to suggest that the idea was absurd.

The local merchants swore he was alone and that he shopped as a single man would: nothing elaborate, simple food, small quantities.

Georgie was suffering from male pattern baldness, the wig block in the room, might mean they were now looking for him in a disguise.

In the open fields the search was progressing quickly He watched as some of the teams completed their allocated grid pattern, consulted their maps, checked their bearings and set out on their new trajectory.

The teams in the woods and in the heavy overgrown gardens were slower, hampered by the years of neglect and growth that could hide an army of murdered bodies.

Now and then his heart missed a beat as he thought he heard the cry yodelling across the fields and through the woods. But the call never came, and by evening they had established that the estate, house and outbuildings were empty, and that of Bowen and Gaffney very little trace remained, of their stay at Bowen Court.

Chapter 39

The girl who brought the tea was young and now that Grammy scrutinized her properly, was dressed in a very odd way indeed. It was as if she had come from her toilet with the job incomplete: her shift in place but her outer garment discarded and forgotten.

Grammy was remembering that at first, in her day, dress had not been so informal. Now a general revolt had begun. The youth were signifying their rebellion, by wearing short dresses - skirts and outlandish coloured clothes, and make-up: and girls, she would hesitate to call them young ladies, were smoking in public.

The tea was unsatisfactory, some blend she was sure: a cheap blend sold in Teashops. She would normally have complained, but a part of her was scolding: keep quiet, don't draw attention, go and find George. He will know what to do: find the boy.

When Grammy again inquired at the house, she was told that Mister Bowen had not returned yet and that in light of the lateness of the hour was unlikely to return today, perhaps she should try again tomorrow.

The giggly secretary would have said, in her crude vernacular that she told the Old biddy to clear off. Bowen was missing. Come back tomorrow he might be here tomorrow. Bloody unlikely as that was!

A night back in her own home, in her own bed, would refresh her for another attempt to locate George tomorrow. She would go to the station, board the train, and likely when she arrived back in Bowen Court, the boy would be there fretting about her.

Yes, of course, that was where she would find him. Her decision was made and her spirits were restored. She would return home immediately. She set out, to find a hackney driver, who would deliver her back to the station.

Detective Sergeant Shay Fanahan Dog Minder: that was how he now regarded himself. He was really shagged, he wouldn't dare call in any favours to get off this detail, because he didn't want anyone to know about it.

He considered giving Blind Biddy, his mobile number and asking her to phone him if she was going out, and to wait while he came over. If he did that and went to Milo's and waited out the interval and had a drink, she or the bloody dog, was sure to sniff him out.

What was it? When God let you down on one sense he made up for it by making the others sharper. True enough he reasoned I saw a man the other day with a short leg and the other one was definitely longer.

Shaggin' dog's - shaggin'- dinner of a job. He groaned and settled back in the car seat, and I can't even doss and have a sleep, because if she comes out to go somewhere, I have to see her and go over. Maybe if I get a Big Mac and hang it on the door the mutt will wait for me.

Whoops! Here we go. Must be time to go out and get the fish fingers for the tea.

"Missus Greene, I'm over here," he called as he clicked the key lock, and heard the noise of the locks engaging.

"Detective Fanahan," she answered, "I'm just out to get something for the tea. I'm sorry about this I told Bob – Superintendent Tyrell that it's a waste of time. I'm sure Sheba is just getting old and cranky."

At the sound of her name, the dog wagged her tail and

continued to lead the way to the shops on High Street.

The blood flea-bag has a smile on her puss, he thought as an itchy feeling started below his right shoulder. He raised his left hand across his chest , over his shoulder and through his coat scratched his back, but the itch was not soothed.

"I'll be just behind you, close behind you."

He loosened his tie and jammed his hand down his back, under his shirt, and raked his nails, in satisfaction, as he conquered the itch.

He moved out on the pavement and watched each man who approached, and quickly checked the dog for any reaction.

Shaggin waste of time, waste of shaggin time, he railed each time he completed the motions. He started to call the people names in his head as he checked them. *Beer belly -clear. Wavy teeth and straight hair – clear. Syrup-of-figs - clear.*

Feck! His day dream was interrupted by the low growl. He turned. The dog had stopped, rock steady on the path, the hairs on her lower neck and upper back were standing stiff, a low guttural growl forced through the bared teeth.

"Steady, steady. Act natural Missus Greene. Leave it to me."

He checked the people who were approaching, isolating and noting the men, blanking out the rest, *men first, women and children last.* Check the men. In the corner of his eye he saw her: his mind would have eliminated her, if she had not stopped terrified, staring at the dog.

Leave her! It's a man I'm looking for. The stupid auld biddy is just reacting to the mutt. Probably bitten as a child or her auld fellow always wanted to do it doggy style.

Forget her look for a man.

The dog was straining forward pulling the handler along the path.

"Feck!" *She is after the auld biddy. This is all fecked up! What will I do if the mutt bites her. What if she turns out to be someone's granny. Shit! I'd better step in.*

"Hold back the dog Missus Greene, It's all right Granny. The dog won't bite you."

He approached the old lady, who was now cowering against a building, a look of horror and fear grossly distorting her features.

Shit look at that gear, She's like something out of a painting.

"It's OK! It's OK!" Slowly, carefully, he approached, arms outstretched before him.

Make yourself small Fanahan, non threatening. A friend who will help. Move very slowly. Shit! I think I know this Auld Biddy from somewhere. Christ No! Not even drunk - out of my mind - would I give her one. Not if I had a bag of 'em! That much Guinness doesn't exist!

Shay had been a long time on the streets. He had been in a lot of situations that were a danger to him, places and occasions where he felt threatened. Sometimes he had even been in danger of being shot, or harmed in other ways. Though this appeared to be just an auld biddy afraid of a dog: self preservation took over, he held back.

"Missus Greene," he instructed. "Bring the dog closer now."

He hoped it would happen. He was delighted when the dog feeling the restraint loosening, ran forward, pulling free from the handler.

Before any contact was made, the old dear, screamed and fainter, falling forward onto him. Surprised by the heaviness of the dead-weight hitting him he fell backwards.

Her limp body crashed him onto the pavement, and rolled sideways, lay there not moving, out cold, face up beside him. One of his arms was caught beneath the body and as he rose with his back towards the gathering crowd, his arm came clear and dislodged the wig and the hat, held tight, with a single long hair pin.

A compassion that seldom exerted itself in his hard personality caused him to reach forward to replace the wig. *Poor bitch, she's nearly bald.*

He reached forward and swept the wispy strands, across the temple. *That might help.*

Almost instantly cold sweat rushed into and out through his pores. The face that he thought was familiar, the one that he prayed he hadn't met while drunk now jumped clearly into focus.

The Prick the accountant. The Prick his drinking acquaintance. The Prick the kidnapper. The Prick the serial killer. The Prick who could land him in a big pile of cowshite, if he didn't handle this carefully.

Shoot The Fucker now. Say you thought he was in disguise, and had a gun and was trying to shoot the dog.

"Ah! Feck I'm bollixed and I'm really bollixed if I'm thinking like that."

Chapter 40

At last! Bishop Mahon felt his heart beat quicken, hands shaking he moved the mouse and opened the email, quickly scanning the message. It was the one he had been awaiting. 'Please present yourself and consignment documents at office of Ford and White Freight Agent, 23 Cill Malogue Street, at 2100 hours today for collection. Bring only Airwaybill Papers. Our reference is S3XNES'.

He recalled the drill and worked out what the message was telling him. Go to that address at eight o'clock tonight, one hour before 2100 hours, be alone.

The rest of the plan, provided O'Neill was satisfied that he was alone and was playing the game by the rules, was that a car, a white ford, would come past. If it had a sticker in the back window for the pop group SEXINESS, or something similar, that he would recognize from the reference number, he was to follow it to the meeting place.

This was how it had happened in the past. When O'Neill and his fellow terrorists were involved it had always worked and he had always been given safe conduct.

The war was over and he had no reason to suspect that this time things would be any different. He would get the priest and deliver him to the nearest Garda Station and tell the media he had been negotiating for a safe release all the time.

Now he had decisions to make. Would he wear his best suit: dress in his Bishop's Finery? Maybe he would root out an old camouflage jacket and wear that. Don't be foolish – best bib and tucker for the media.

Traonach had been told all he needed to know: that this was a different operation than just handing over the priest. If he was surprised when The Boss told him he was going to kill Bishop Mahon – he kept it to himself.

Sonny knew it was going to be a tricky plan. To lure Mahon into the trap, at some stage he would have to see the priest. If the priest saw and recognized Mahon, he would have to be killed as well. He didn't deserve that. The only blame he shared in this was the blame of his community, The Church , and its indifference to the crimes that were committed in its name. Suffer the little children to come onto me. The sins of the father. Those thoughts went through his mind, entertaining it, he smiled as it came to him: the good thief and the bad thief, one on either side of the cross. One had stolen innocence, the other had stolen nothing: as far as he knew, and had nothing to answer for. But isn't life a bitch, sometimes.

Feckit Gaffney doesn't deserve any of this, or to be mixed up in this, he's just another one of the innocent.

What will she think when she finds out? When it breaks in the papers. She always understood in the past, but that was war, her war as well as mine.

Traonach knew to leave The Boss alone to his thoughts at a time like this, the temper would be short, the nerves on edge. Sometimes he wondered if O'Neill was still cut out for this kind of thing.

If he worried to much about the violence the killings now, was he was starting to worry about his soul?

He had seen it happen: evil killers getting religion and starting to worry about their stains of sin. With compassion they were feck-all use to anyone, except the do-gooder.

O'Neill asked him "What did you do with Anto and the girl?"

"What?"

"Anto and the girl where are they? Have you got them stashed?"

"Yes."

"Get them. Bring them tonight. I have plans for them. Anto will come in handy, that bollix owes me, as well. Mess him up a bit. Make it look like he was well and truly crucified – for his sins."

Chapter 41

Jim Gaffney was light-headed now that he was free. Even on the journey when instructed to review his position on information gained in confession. He still believed that the trip would end in some Garda Barracks: where he would soon be able to leave, and contact, and comfort his family.

He had decided The Church could wait for his reappearance. In fact he had some real thinking to do, before deciding if he would return to his duties.

Being kidnapped, brought home to him the realization, that he had not really lived yet: Despite all his training, and the times he thought he had been of help in preparing his dying parishioners for the next life – he was not as ready as he might have been to follow them.

They were travelling back towards Dublin, but just as they reached the outskirts: in a lay-by off the carriageway, he was directed to leave the car, and get into the back of a windowless van. After that, the weaving stop and start trip, disorientated him again. When he was taken out in a yard and pushed into a house: once again he had no idea of where he was.

The only conclusion he could come to was that he had not been freed as expected. He believed he had been taken out of the frying pan and placed firmly into the fire.

He sat at the table and looked around the dingy, dirty room, and in despair wondered how long more will I be a captive?

How long more do I have before I know the answer to that question?

How long more do I have to live?

In all the time of his incarceration so far, this was the first time he wondered if he could still get out of this predicament alive.

The door opened. The tall monk his facial features indiscernible beneath the hood of a brown habit, wearing sandals showing bare feet, entered the room. He handed over an identical robe.

"Wear this, Father. It will only be for a while. We will get your other clothes cleaned up before you meet the media."

He waited while Jim changed.

Chapter 42

After his crucifixion Anto and the girl had been taken from the railway line and kept locked away in a small room in the warehouse that housed O'Neill's drug operation in Ireland.

They had been given rags to bind their wounds and were fed each day, they even got a small supply of drugs. It kept them quiet and docile.

For the first few hours after the beating neither of them cared where they were, or even if they were alive.

Gradually, over a short period of time, that thought pushed its way upwards into their awareness: we are still alive.

Now the girl shook and slobbered again, pissed herself and if she had any faecal matter in her bowels would have shit herself as well.

The nightmare was back. She was lying beside the tracks again. Herself and Anto had been taken from their room and thrown into the back of a van and brought back here: to where it happened.

The big man was there waiting.

He made Anto wear the black suit and when the other car and the van came, he pulled the bandages off Anto and made him stand there: his wrist bleeding again.

They were up on the bank above her. He kept telling Anto to be still, and kept promising him that he was safe and wouldn't be harmed if he did what he was told.

When the other man in the black suit and the two Monks came walking down the tracks, on the sleepers, and when they were near, he told them to stop, and stay away a bit.

"They crucified him," he said loudly and told Anto to raise his hands, "they crucified him for the sins of the father, your sins." He added.

The other man in the black suit stopped. He just stood there for a moment. Casually he moved his body and put one of his hands into his trouser pocket. His coat front was swept back by his arm, and she saw the purple and the cross, as it flashed, in the rays of the dying sun.

"What's this all about? What sins?"

The big man said, "The sins you have committed. Father."

"We are all sinners. You know I prefer Bishop."

"I know who you are and I know what you did. Father."

"Feck it, O'Neill! What's this all about? Hand over the priest and let me get on with it."

"We are not finished, Father."

"Lets get on with it, and cut the father shit. I'm not any ones father"

"No?"

They all detected the menace at the way the single word was shouter and repeated, louder, higher. "NO?"

Again, softer. The venom remained.

"No! Think back Chaplain. Think back Army Chaplain. Think Lourdes. Think of young innocent girls from the farms. Think of how you screwed them and pissed off, back to the comfortable life. Left them to pick up the pieces of their lives. Being screwed by a priest! Jesus you didn't become the bastard I know today. You were always a bastard, Mahon."

"Feck it. That was a long time ago. They knew what they were doing. They could have stopped me at any time. Most of them were mad for it. Come on give me the priest and let me away, and stop this shit about what I did in the past. You are not an innocent yourself."

She watched as The Bishop tried to walk forward and get neared to the big man. One of the monks shot him in the leg. No warning, just shot him in the leg, and he fell over.

Anto had difficulty standing upright. The Boss told him to stand or he would shoot him dead. The wounds in his feet and the blood that was flowing from the wounds in his wrists made him light headed. He tried to stay standing but he failed and fell over.

For the girl the nightmare continued to play itself out almost like a film. Across the screen she saw Anto trying to stand upright, The Boss beside him, she heard Anto 'I'll try Boss."

Just a short distance away The Bishop was starting to fall over and the smoke was coming out of the arm of the monk's robe. The other monk just stood there.

Mahon tried to shout. The shock of the bullet hitting his lower leg came first. Then he saw the puff of earth jumping upwards, about a half meter in front and to the side, of where he was standing. Shock and the realization of what had happened, made him aware of the burning pain

He tried to stand, but the shattered muscle and bone could not hold his weight and he fell sideways and over the railway track. The pain, shock and outrage reached his consciousness and as his head crashed against the stones he blacked out.

O'Neill watched him fall. "Lift him back onto the sleepers. Put him in the middle on his back. We'll crucify him."

"You can't crucify him," Traonach said. "That's our

trademark, in the war and now in the drugs. Besides, you'll make a martyr out of him if you do."

"Well what the Feck do I do with him, in your opinions, Smartarses?" O'Neill shuffled and looked around. His temper was starting to overtake his reason. Next, they knew, would come frustration. Then he was was likely to make a quick decision, and take action.

"I can't let him go. He has to pay!"

"So just kill him."

"No. He has to suffer, like she did. He has to suffer."

"Addict him, Make him dependent?"

"When he got the chance the bastard would do cold turkey and beat it."

"Feck it Shane we can't stand here all night talking about it. Do fecken something."

"Do what he did," Traonach said slowly, "take something he values, like he did."

"Fecken what though?"

Traonach walked over the railway line, down the embankment, and reaching down lifted the girl to her feet and brought her up to where the conversation had stopped.

O'Neill asked again, "Take fecken what?"

"He's a bishop, and he likes being a bishop. A Prince of the church. Take that away from him, let him live with that. Take that. And it's better than taking his life."

Francis Sylvester Mahon was talking to God, who was telling him he was doing a good job, looking after the flock very well and was a credit to his Church.

God was asking him where he wanted to sit and indicating with his glowing white hand and his glowing white sleeve towards a table that was laden with food and drink. Around this table the Apostles sat enjoying the feast.

Only the middle seat was empty and God was gently pushing him towards that. All the Apostles were smiling and calling him to come.

From the corner of his eye he saw another figure lurking half hidden, framed against the brightness. "Judas?"

The figure moved out of the glare and he saw O'Neill looking down at him.

"Yes Judas. You're getting the full picture. Aren't you? This is my show. Isn't it boys. Let's do it now."

Mahon knew they were helping him those Angels who carried the stings that took away his pain. He slept again and Mary Magdalene ministered to him. She wiped his tears and his feet with her hair. He could feel it brush against his nakedness.

He knew he had died of his wound and this was Heaven. It was peaceful and they ministered to him as a Prince – all his desires were fulfilled, any pleasure he had ever dreamed about he dreamed about now again.

After a while in this paradise Bishop Mahon, came to the conclusion that if this was heaven he had been wrong about it all his life. If this was Hell: he could put up with it for eternity.

Chapter 43

Each Sunday morning, after he had attended Mass, and was at home again in the quiet after breakfast, Bob Tyrell sat in the front room and read the Sunday Papers.

Today they had several stories to tell. Chief among them on all front pages were the photographs of Bishop Mahon and the young woman, or Bishop Mahon and the young boy, or the Bishop and the Threesome.

You picked the paper and you read their story.

A BLESSING WITH THE BISHOPS CROZIER was the caption on one photo, with a small blacked out block, but still clearly showing a young girl having oral sex with Bishop Mahon.

There were other photographs of The Bishop in Amsterdam in Dam Square. Walking through the Red Light District and taking and laughing face-on to an unknown pimp, who had his back towards the camera.

This pimp it was alleged had supplied Mahon with young women and boys and organized orgies for him. Sources close to the man, who was also a small operator in the Drug Trade, confirmed that he was unaware that his client was a Catholic Cleric.

When he learned that the man who called himself Ahab was really Bishop Mahon, the pimp was so disgusted that he decided to confront him.

Mahon had become suspicious that the meeting was a trap of some kind. He came armed with a gun, started a shoot out, shot the pimp and was himself injured.

Associates of the pimp provided the press with the story of Mahon's hidden life. Church Authorities were quoted as saying that The Bishop had been sent away for treatment and was unavailable for comment.

Bob scanned the other editions, now and his eye was drawn to some of the more outlandish accounts of Mahon's fall from grace.

Two altar boys who served mass for Bishop Mahon when he was a curate have also made allegations of sexual misconduct against him. Several women also claimed that when they were on pilgrimage in Lourdes, that they were date raped by the bishop, then an Army Chaplain. They alleged that he used a drug to spike their drinks that made them compliant with his evil desires.

It was also reported that Mahon when travelling on official church duties, used his Bishops Raiment to avoid being checked at Irish Customs. He was acting as a Mule for a continental based drugs smuggler. The money he received for these consignments has been traced to a Hong Kong bank. Mahon was an egomaniac who kept a record of some of his escapades in poetic form. One of these doggerel verses was received by this newspaper and is reproduced here.

Bishop Mahon counts the money Sunday afternoon.
He builds it up in little piles and sings a funny tune.
The money in that LITTLE pile belongs to the Holy
Sea. The money in the OTHER pile belongs to clever
ME.
When it is my time to quit. I'll settle in Hong Kong,
where lots of little toy-boys can squat upon my dong.
I am a Holy Bishop of the Holy Sea. Looking out for all
the flock, especially FOR ME.

Looking out for all the flock, especially FOR ME.

The money in that LITTLE pile belongs to the Holy Sea. The money in the OTHER pile belongs to clever ME.

I am a Holy Bishop of the Holy Sea. Looking out for all the flock, especially FOR ME.

Chapter 44

Detective Inspector Shay Fanahan, the recent recipient of an almost unknown award in the Garda Siochana, a promotion for outstanding detective work in the field, sat in the only Public House in his home village of Rathmor, a freshly filled pint of Guinness and an empty glass that up to recently had held a full double measure of Irish Whiskey, before him on the counter.

He unfolded the most recent edition of the local weekly Galway Centurion, his home town paper and found what he was looking for.

Father Jim Gaffney, the Priest, who up to recently, had been held captive, by a crazed serial killer, was liberated safe and well today by the astute detection work of Garda Seamus Fanahan, a native of Rathmor, Galway.

Garda Fanahan is a son of the late, Seamus Fanahan of Beglive, and the late Brigid Fanahan (nee Morrissey) of Rathmor.

Garda Fanahan, who is down home on a few days of well earned rest, told this reporter, exclusively, the whole story in his own words.

I was lucky, that the description we got from an eye witness was so accurate and specific that I was able to trace the kidnapper's movements and to recognize and apprehend him on the street.

In the charge room later in a short time I gained his confidence and the prisoner came to trust me and revealed where he had been holding the hostage. I was able to lead my team in the rescue and we re-leased Father Gaffney without any further delay.

I just thank God that I was able to find and apprehend the killer before he did away with the priest. We know he intended to kill the priest because he had a grave dug and ready.

My sympathies also go to the family and friends of his eleven victims. I am just glad that good Garda work solved this case that was still open after so long a time.

All I want to do now is have a few days relaxing back down home, meeting a few school pals, that I have kept in touch with and do a little fishing.

Fishing my arse, all I want to do is sit here and let these feckers see that I have been a success ever since I climbed out of this shit pile they call home.

Feck Me! I deserve all this. I held me nerve well when The Prick popped up dressed as his granny and nearly fecked it all up. I wonder, if I would have had the balls to shoot him, if he hadn't been loopy, bawling and pissing in his trousers. No pissing in his granny's knickers when I recognized him.

Well he's away now with the other numb-sculls and loopers and the quacks say he will remain there in his little dream world for a long time, maybe forever.

Shit ! It's hard to believe that when I was trying to get some info out of him in the charge room, and having no luck at all. He kept slobbering and whispering to me about dignity and respect and him calling me Sir, and Constable, saying he always respected the Rule of Law, obeyed the Civil Authorities.

Then I got the bloody phone call telling me where the priest was and I was able to tie the two in nicely and say that he whispered the location to me in an unguarded moment. And as they say everything came up roses.

He smiled and replied "Irish. A double," when another one of the locals stopped to clap him on the back and say "Well done Shamie. We're all proud of ye. Will ya have a drink? Tell us all about it. Sure yer Auld Fella would be proud of ya, He would indeed."

Feck them, if they want the story, first hand, let them pay the price. The local swallowed hard. "Mikie. A double Irish for Shamie when you're ready."

From the corner of his eye Fanahan saw Grocer Parkie Egan approaching. This bollix was a right bully at school. Egan shook his hand and clapped him on the back. As if he was anticipating the next question Fanahan said. "A double Irish and a Pint would go down well, Parkie. Thanks. And how have you been keepin'?"

As far as Bob Tyrell was concerned the case would not be solved until all the bodies had been identified and handed over to the relatives for burial. So far four bodies waited for positive identification and he was determined to drive the forensic team hard for solutions.

They would never be able to bring Georgie into court. In fact with each passing day the specialists were telling him that the personality of Grammy, or The Duchess, as they now called her was becoming the permanent and dominant entity.

Without the initials on the trees we would never be able to work out who he had killed.

Fanahan did well out of the case. I'll be OK myself when it all finishes. I might even think of early retirement. Go out at the top.

Now what I need to do is go shopping and get a reward for the one who really solved the case. A nice big juicy, chewy bone, for Sheba.

Epilogue

"Nurse."

"Doctor Reilly."

"That man Edwards, the one with the colon cancer. Did he pay his bill?"

"I'll check. Doctor"

"Doctor, I can't find any record of a visit by Mr. Edwards."

"Check again. He had tests and has colon cancer. He came in and I gave him the news."

"No, Doctor. We have not had a visit from George Edwards."

"Yes. We had. The accountant fellow."

"Doctor that's George Edward Bowen."

"Shit! What did he have?"

"Piles. Doctor."

"Piles! Not cancer!"

"That's correct Doctor."